WDB

THE ALIAS MAN

THE ALIAS MAN

Bill Pronzini

Walker & Company ✳ New York

First published in the United States of America in 2004 by
Walker Publishing Company, Inc.

Published simultaneously in Canada by Fitzhenry and Whiteside,
Markham, Ontario L3R 4T8

For information about permission to reproduce selections from
this book, write to Permissions, Walker & Company,
104 Fifth Avenue, New York, New York 10011.

Library of Congress Cataloging-in-Publication Data available upon request
ISBN: 0-8027-3381-6

Book design by M.J. DiMassi

Visit Walker & Company's Web site at www.walkerbooks.com

Printed in the United States of America

2 4 6 8 10 9 7 5 3 1

For Marcia

Who turned on a couple of lights while
I was stumbling around in the dark.

There is a smile of love,
And there is a smile of deceit,
And there is a smile of smiles
In which these two smiles meet.
—WILLIAM BLAKE

When he is best, he is a little worse
than a man, and when he is worst, he
is little better than a beast.
—SHAKESPEARE, The
Merchant of Venice

The Alias Man

Friday, May 9–Sunday, May 18

Jessie

Santa Fe, New Mexico

THE lobby bar at La Fonda was open-sided and dark. From where she sat at a corner table, she could watch people scurrying back and forth across the worn old tiles, people entering the courtyard restaurant for a late lunch. Outside, on the Plaza and the narrow streets leading away from it, more people would be flowing and gawking. Tourists like herself exclaiming over the Palace of Governors ("the oldest continuously used public building in the United States, built in 1820, now our state museum") and the Saint Francis Cathedral ("built in 1869 and named after the patron saint of Santa Fe"). Buying souvenirs and clothing and Native American jewelry and southwestern art. Enjoying themselves in this city that dripped history and charm, in one of the prettiest settings in the country. How could you *not* enjoy yourself in Santa Fe?

I'm not, she thought.

This isn't working, dammit.

She sipped some of her margarita. Her second margarita. She'd intended to have just one and then lunch, but the first hadn't made her want food, it had invited a second. Feeling the effects already. It was very warm for early May, and the high altitude lowered your tolerance for alcohol. One more, and she'd be ripped. At one o'clock in the afternoon.

Maybe she'd have one more.

She watched the people hurrying and scurrying, and felt isolated and alone among them. Darrin, of course. But Darrin had been gone almost seven months now, and how long could you go on grieving? Brenda had said that to her last week—a perfectly good question, the kind that brooked no argument. "You've always had a yen to visit New Mexico," Brenda had said. "For heaven's sake, why don't you? I'd join you, but there's just too much to do at the gallery right now. No reason you can't go by yourself, is there? I mean, you're a big girl, Jessie, you're edging up on the big four-oh. It's time already."

Yes, right. It was time. And so here she was in Santa Fe. One and a half days down, two and a half more to go. Then three more after that in Taos. Five and a half days left on her one-week getaway. And it wasn't working. Already she had begun to retreat, to wish she were back home and puttering in the big old barn among her musty antiques.

A mistake, this trip. Knew it would be, did it anyway at Brenda's urging. You think it'll be easier to be alone among strangers, in new and attractive surroundings, but it isn't. Fallacy. It's much easier to keep up the pretense that you're mending, adjusting, moving ahead, among supportive friends and relatives in familiar surroundings. The familiar was the perfect hiding place: After a while you could convince yourself that you weren't really hiding at all.

She sipped; the second margarita was almost gone. Very good it was, too. To order a third, or not to order a third? Let us consider carefully, Jessie. Oh, all right, you talked me into it. She signaled to the waitress. Abracadabra, and another frosty, salt-rimmed glass appeared magically in front of her.

The waitress wore a large turquoise and coral ring that prompted Jessie to think of the ring she'd bought earlier in one of the shops. She retrieved the box from her purse for another look. Egg-shaped turquoise stone, slightly flawed, in a hammered silver setting. It would be a good match for the earrings Darrin had given her two . . . no, three Christmases ago. Most men had no taste in jewelry or women's clothing, but he—

Darrin again.

Damn you, Darrin, why did you have to die on me like that?

His voice seemed to echo faintly in her mind. Come on now,

she imagined him saying, I didn't die *on* you. Remember how we always joked about that? The perfect epitaph for a lusty bugger like Darrin Keene: He came, and he went.

Not funny, she thought.

It happened after we made love, anyway, his voice said. Not during.

You were only forty-three. Forty-three!

Congenital heart disease. Runs in my family—father dead at fifty-two, his father at forty-nine. We knew there was a risk. We talked about it, remember?

But we never really thought it would happen. I didn't, anyway.

Life's a crapshoot, to coin a phrase. Shit happens. Get over it, kiddo.

How? And no clichés, please.

Brooding isn't the answer.

Don't you think I know that? Brooding isn't the answer, work isn't the answer, friends aren't the answer, New Mexico and margaritas aren't the answer. What's the answer?

You could get laid.

Shut up. That's not what I need.

Isn't it? After seven long months. You know you're an attractive woman. Wouldn't be too hard to meet a fella.

I don't want to meet anybody!

It'd be a hell of a lot better than holding imaginary dialogues with your dead husband. If you don't think so, then maybe you're cracking up.

Well, maybe I am.

Bullshit, kiddo. You're not one of these weepy women who can't handle stress or crisis. Strong, always in control. Why can't you deal with this situation as you've dealt with others? Get over it, get past it, get on with your life?

I don't know. If I knew, I would—

"Excuse me."

The voice, deep and male, came from above and close beside her. She blinked, twisting her head up, squinting. At first all she saw was the shape of him, a looming silhouette against the light from the lobby; then he moved sideways, and she had a clearer look. Early to mid forties, lean, wavy-haired, smiling. Vaguely familiar . . .

"I'm sorry," he said, "I didn't mean to startle you."

"You didn't. I was . . . woolgathering."

"I recognized you, and you looked a little pensive, so I thought I'd come over and say hello."

"Pensive?" She shook her head; the margaritas had filled it with fuzz. "I don't think we've met."

"No, we haven't. I saw you at Hazelrigg's earlier."

"Hazelrigg's?"

"The gallery over on Palace. You were looking at one of the paintings."

"Oh," she said, "yes. The acrylic landscape."

"*Devil's Wind*. You seemed to like it."

"Actually, no. I found it . . . disturbing."

"How so?"

"The way the storm clouds were drawn to resemble death's-heads and goblins. It made me feel cold."

"Exactly the reaction the artist intended to evoke. You're not an admirer of the macabre in art, I take it."

"Not really. Are you?"

"Yes, if it's well done and carries a message. Bosch's *Bird-Headed Monster*, Picasso's *Guernica*, Goya's *Madhouse* and *Witches' Sabbath*. The best of Dalishar's work, *Devil's Wind* and one called *The Devouring*, have the same surrealist style and flavor."

"Well, each to his own taste," she said. "Dalishar—that's an odd name."

"Unique is a better word. He's a unique man."

"A local artist?"

"He divides his time between Santa Fe and San Francisco. He's had shows elsewhere as well."

"It sounds as though you know him."

"I do. Would you like to meet him?"

She opened her mouth, closed it again when she couldn't think of an appropriate response. Damn magaritas. Damn fuzz.

"May I sit down?"

"Well . . ."

He drew back one of the other chairs and stood with his hand on its back, watching her, smiling and waiting.

Meet a fella.

No, she thought. "All right," she heard herself say.

When he was seated across from her, she saw that he had a kind of Lincolnesque face, all knobs and sharp angles, the cheekbones like miniature crags. It might have been an austere face except for laugh lines that bracketed a wide mouth, mild and gentle brown eyes. Not a handsome face, but an interesting and attractive one. And that wavy hair, thick and black except for white wings at the temples, was beautiful. She'd thought the same, fleetingly, at Hazelrigg's. He'd caught her looking at him there and smiled at her; she couldn't remember if she'd smiled back.

"My name is Court," he said, "Frank Court."

"Jessie Keene."

"That's a nice name. Jessie."

Again she couldn't think of anything to say.

"Where are you from, Jessie?"

"Pennsylvania. Elton."

"A town I'm not familiar with."

"It's a village, really. In Bucks County, near Doylestown."

"Pretty country. What do you do there?"

"I have an antique shop. Keene's Antiques."

"Ah. What do you specialize in?"

"Victorian and Pennsylvania Dutch furniture. Glassware, pottery, lighting fixtures, the usual miscellany."

"Paintings?"

"No. My best friend operates a gallery in Elton. Any good old canvases I pick up at auction go to Brenda for resale."

He studied her for a moment. "Are you with anyone, Jessie?"

"I don't . . . You mean here in Santa Fe?"

"Husband, boyfriend, girlfriend, maiden aunt?"

"No one. I'm a widow."

"Oh? Recent?"

"Seven months."

"I'm sorry," he said. "I mean that."

"Thank you."

"Would you care to talk about it? I'm a good listener."

She shook her head, reached out to the third margarita; but instead of drawing it closer, she pushed it farther away. She'd had enough. Enough alcohol, enough fuzz, enough self-pity.

He said, "Potent drinks, margaritas, on a hot afternoon at this altitude."

"So I'm finding out."

"Especially on an empty stomach. Or have you had lunch?"

"Not yet."

"Neither have I. There's an excellent little restaurant half a block from here called the Shed. Have you been yet?"

"No."

"They make the best sopaipillas in Santa Fe. Use their own special honey—the owner's hobby is beekeeping. Will you join me?"

"Well . . ."

"Please do. Dutch treat, if you prefer."

She heard herself say, "Why are you so interested, Mr. Court?"

"Frank. In lunch? I'm hungry, and I imagine you are too."

"Not in lunch. In me."

"Shouldn't I be?"

"I'm . . . not a casual pickup."

He raised an eyebrow. "Of course you're not. Did I give the impression I thought you were?"

"No, but—"

"If you'd like me to leave—"

She said quickly, "I didn't mean to insult you."

"You didn't. I admit to a weakness for slim beautiful blonds with blue eyes, and when I saw you in Hazelrigg's—"

"Gray," she said.

"Pardon?"

"My eyes. They're more gray than blue."

"Not in this light. Not from where I sit."

His gaze held hers; his brown eyes were guileless. "And I'm not beautiful," she said, "not by any stretch. My mouth's too big, for one thing."

"Nonsense. You are beautiful. And I have no ulterior motive in saying so."

Uh-huh, she thought, I've heard that line before. And then realized she'd spoken the words aloud.

"It's not a line, Jessie. I'm attracted to you, I don't deny that. All initial male-female attraction is sex-based, after all. But that's as far as it goes."

"For now, you mean."

"For now. Do you find *me* attractive?"

She blinked at the question. "I don't know you."

"You don't have to know a person to feel an attraction to them. First impression . . . yes or no?"

"Yes," she said, with only the slightest hesitation.

"Good. Excellent. So there's no reason why we shouldn't have lunch together."

"I suppose not."

"Or see each other again after that, if we enjoy each other's company. If you're interested in meeting Dalishar, I'd like you to be my guest at a party he's giving night after tomorrow, to celebrate the sale of two of his paintings. He has an interesting and diverse circle of friends."

"Including you."

"Including me. As a matter of fact, I'm staying with him this trip."

"Trip? You don't live in Santa Fe?"

"San Francisco. I'm here on business. Well, a combination of business and pleasure."

"Are you an artist too?"

"Don't I wish. But I have no talent of my own, I'm afraid. I'm strictly an aficionado. I met Dalishar at a gallery in San Francisco, at one of his showings." He sighed. "Computers," he said.

"Excuse me?"

"That's my business. I sell computer software. Not very glamorous, and it requires more travel than I like, but it pays well. And allows me to indulge my passion for art."

Her eyes shifted briefly to his left hand resting on the table; the ring finger was bare.

He said, smiling, "No, I'm not married. No wife, no kids, no dependents except for a schlefflera that my landlady waters for me when I'm away."

She laughed. She felt at ease with him now, and it had nothing to do with the liquor—the fuzz was mostly gone. She liked him. Personable, candid, and that wavy hair and those gentle eyes . . . except for his taste in art, what was there not to like? He might well have the usual male intentions, but what if he did? Maybe her inner voice was right and it *was* time she got laid. And maybe Frank Court was the man for the job. If they both got exactly what they needed, there was no harm in that, was there?

"The Shed, then, Jessie?" he asked. "I really am pretty hungry."

She reached for her purse. "Me, too. Starving."

Sarah

Vancouver, British Columbia

S HE was going to have to sell the bookshop.

Either that, or marry David.

There was no use trying to deny it any longer; the bills and bank statements and income records made the situation all too clear. Crisis point, fast approaching. Yet another crisis to be met and dealt with in the least difficult way possible.

When she closed Bright Lights at six o'clock, she drove from Gastown to Hastings and merged with the sluggish flow of Friday-evening commuters crossing the Granville Street Bridge. Traffic thinned considerably after the West Van exits; she continued north past Horseshoe Bay and the Nanaimo ferry, and on up the coast. To the west Howe Sound was dark and choppy, Vancouver Island invisible behind a screen of mist; the towering ramparts of the Coast Range rose six thousand cloud-packed feet to the east. Depressing vistas in weather like this, but she barely noticed tonight. Driving relaxed her, helped her think. Better a long drive than the flat on West Tenth. If she'd gone there, the first thing she'd have done was pour herself a large Scotch and then maybe keep right on pouring, and she'd been drinking too much lately. Besides, the flat wasn't home. Home, the last real home she'd had, had been the Kitsilano house she'd shared with Scott, and it was gone nearly three years now, sold off at not much profit to keep the bookshop staggering along. She'd loved that house; giving it up had added a new layer of pain and displacement to her life. Something else she'd lost, as well as one of the other crises met and dealt with.

She considered the two options facing her now. The first would be painful, another act of giving up. The shop was her one refuge—always plenty to do there, and the scent and texture and visual appeal of books, as well as their contents, were a comfort. But business was way off, had been since the events of September 11, 2001, and the downturn in tourism from the States that followed. She was barely making ends meet now. Unless there was a radical upswing this summer, enough increase in profits to last through the off-season—and that wasn't likely—she would be too deeply mired in debt to dig herself out without help.

Another bank loan was out unless she had a cosigner. David would do that for her, or make her an outright loan; all she had to do was ask. His family law practice was among the most successful in the city. But realistically, either kind of loan was likely to be no more than a postponing of the inevitable—a temporary plug in a very weak dike. If the shop failed anyway, she would never be able to repay him.

The same was true if she let him buy a half-interest in Bright Lights, as he'd indicated once he was willing to do. Her pride wouldn't allow that, either. She hated the idea of presuming on a friendship, accepting what was really an act of charity. It was unfair to David as well.

If she had to give up her independence in order to keep the bookshop, she might as well give him what he yearned for in return. Quid pro quo. Option number two: Marry him. He was in love with her; he'd told her so several times, already asked her once to be his wife in that hopeful, hungry, worshipful way of his. He wouldn't make any demands on her, wouldn't expect her to change. She could keep the shop, and share his upscale lifestyle in West Van, and never again have any financial worries.

She didn't love him, but did that really matter? She cared for him; he was a good man, a good friend, a good companion. A good and considerate lover, too. She'd already been to bed with him three times, hadn't she? All she'd be doing was making a casual, sporadic arrangement permanent. A few words and a piece of paper, no big deal.

Except that it was. Marriage for money, a business proposition—it would make her feel like a whore. That was bad enough, but the real sticking point was Scott. Scott Collins, the only man she'd ever loved.

What if, by some miracle, Scott was still alive?

Dim, foolish hope after four years. Enormous odds against it. She knew that, accepted it; had lost her faith in the possibility long ago. David said it would be simple enough to have Scott declared legally dead, leaving her free to marry again. Yet her whole being balked every time she considered it. Even the last shriveled kernel of hope dies hard. Coping instead of living for four years. Sad, difficult, nowhere relationship with a man who was probably better for her, in the last analysis, than Scott had been. Alone and lonely and facing the loss of the bookshop, the last thing she had left that was important to her, because of an open wound and an emotional short-circuit.

She felt the pain again, that squeezing ache that flared up only occasionally now but still had the power to act on her like a seizure. Why? she thought for the thousandth time. What was Scott doing on Vancouver Island that day, way over by Tofino? Isolated fishing village, wilderness area, no reason for him to be there. His BMW damaged and half submerged beyond a sharp turn. No sign of him inside or out. Nothing to explain what had happened. Missing and presumed dead, body swept out to sea by the strong currents. Implication of suicide, but she'd never believed that; there hadn't been any note, he hadn't seemed despondent or said or done anything that last morning to alarm her. All he'd said was that he "had some business to take care of" and might be gone overnight; then he'd kissed her and gone away for the last time. He'd been distant for a few weeks before that day—the financial setbacks and the problems with his work that had kept them apart so often—but he wasn't the type to become clinically depressed. She'd have intuited it if he were suicidal.

No, you wouldn't, if he didn't want you to. Everybody has two sides, the one they show the world and the one they keep hidden—the dark side.

David had said that to her on more than one occasion, and of course he was right. God knew, she had her dark side. And yes, Scott had had his. Still . . . only a cruel and selfish man would have willfully left his wife such a legacy of pain and uncertainty, and Scott had been neither. Giving, loving . . .

David again, the cold voice of reason: *You've built up an idealized version of your marriage. He was hardly the perfect husband.*

No denying that, either. Scott's stock-market speculation had eaten away thousands of his money and most of what she'd inherited from her father, and nearly sent them into bankruptcy—that had been the main problem. Arguments over that, over his carelessness in cutting back on personal expenditure and paying bills on time, over his heavy travel schedule, over his stubborn refusal to have children, over his tendency to shun social engagements in their last years together. But he'd had so many good points, made her happy more often than he'd made her sad.

If only she knew for certain what had happened that day at Tofino. There was no one who could give her a clue to the truth. He'd had no living relatives, been on his own since the age of sixteen, and had no close friends in Vancouver or anywhere else that he'd ever mentioned. The people he'd worked with were no possible help because his relationships with them had been transitory: he'd been an independent contractor, what he called "a professional middleman" who arranged deals between individuals and companies requiring the services of other individuals and companies, a vague sort of job about which she knew very little.

She might never know the truth about that day.

A light rain began to fall near Shannon Falls, at the northern tip of Howe Sound. She kept on driving, her thoughts tangled now, no longer focused on her financial dilemma. The rain grew heavier and turned into a squall as she approached Squamish. She turned off into the little town. Lighted signs beckoned her on the main street. "Café" was one. In spite of the heater, it was cold in the car; she might as well stop for a cup or two of hot coffee, to give the rain time to move inland before she headed back to Vancouver.

Coffee? She shivered. Her mouth seemed coated with dryness. She drove on toward another sign that read "Tavern."

Morgan

Los Alegres, California

S HE was so distracted, walking out into the teachers' parking lot, that she stepped blindly in front of a moving car.

Brake-locked tires screeched. She jumped backward, pure reflex, and the front bumper barely missed her as the car swerved away and slid to a stop just shy of one of the parked cars opposite. She stood blinking; delayed reaction briefly weakened her knees, set up a pounding in her head. The driver was out now and coming toward her. Alex Hazard. History, art studies, assistant football coach—not such an odd combination in these times, when state and county cutbacks in education forced teachers to wear a number of diverse hats.

"Christ, that was close," he said. "Are you okay?"

Sleepwalker. Automaton. *My body's here but the rest of me is on sabbatical.* Becky Lowenstein's whimsical suggestion for a faculty T-shirt, and not the least bit funny any more. Morgan drew a deep breath before she said, "Yes. I'm sorry, Alex."

"Just as much my fault. Going too fast."

"No, you weren't. I just wasn't paying attention."

He stooped, picked up her briefcase, and handed it to her. She hadn't even realized that she'd dropped it. She forced a smile that felt frozen on her mouth, her head tilted back to look up at him. He was a big man, two or three inches over six feet. His hands were large, freckled; he ran one of them through his bushy tangle of red hair. When you first saw those hands, it was hard to believe they could create such delicate watercolors as he painted in his spare time. Or that a man his size, an ex-football player, would have such a passionate interest in fine art; he and Burt had had spirited discussions and disagreements on the subject on several occasions. Deceptive appearances . . .

". . . sure you're all right, Morgan?"

"What? Oh, yes. Positive."

"I mean in general. You personally."

"Why do you ask?"

"Well, if you don't mind my saying so, you've seemed a little . . . off lately."

"Off?"

"Not yourself. Distant. I'm not the only one who's noticed."

"End-of-term overload, that's all."

"So all's well at home? With you and Burt?"

"Yes, of course," she lied.

Alex studied her for a few seconds, frowning slightly, as if the lie had shown on her face. "All God's chillun got problems," he said. "Helps to talk about them sometimes."

"There's nothing to talk about."

"Well, if you ever feel the need . . ."

"Thanks." Another forced smile. "I'd better go now, Alex. I'm really sorry about this."

"No harm, no foul," he said. "If you promise to look both ways crossing parking lots and streets, I promise to drive more slowly on both."

"Yes, I promise."

She detoured around him, crossed to where her Toyota was slotted. She still felt shaky; she sat there for a time, waiting for it to pass, staring across at the low-slung wings that housed the classrooms of Los Alegres High School. Modernized assembly hall, new gym, refurbished football field and baseball diamond—and cramped, forty-year-old learning facilities in which everything except the computers was old and outdated. Typical small-town school district priorities.

She felt old and outdated herself right now. And alone. Very much alone.

It was hardly a new feeling; she had lived with loneliness all her life, even during the past four years as Mrs. Burton Cord. The connections she'd made in Los Alegres, like the connections in her school years, her previous teaching positions in King City and San Francisco, had been mostly superficial. Men and women gravitated to her, and she welcomed their companionship, but the ones who lingered in her life never became anything more than casual friends. She was too self-contained, too private, for close interpersonal relationships. Parental legacy. Her folks had given her everything growing up in San Diego: training, guidance, a good education, a passion for literature and the arts, material possessions, stolid, dutiful love. Everything but warmth, openness.

She'd never been able to talk to them about anything that mattered to her, how she felt about things, people, herself. Every time she tried, they rerouted her into analytical abstracts—as if they were psychologists treating a mildly disturbed patient. Cold. No, not cold, really. Cold was an extreme, and there were no extremes in the lives of Professors John and Linda Tolliver. Tepid was more apt. The Tepid Tollivers.

Not their daughter, though. Somehow their lukewarm genes had combined to produce an intense offspring who had emotions to burn, emotions too often volatile and conflicted. And yet she was without the internal makeup to allow her to share them with others. She'd tried, God knew. With acquaintances, professors, counselors, even an actual psychologist. Couldn't open up to any of them. Even felt compelled to indulge in a series of small lies and circumlocutions with the psychologist to keep parts of herself hidden.

Now, more than ever, she needed someone to confide in. There were plenty of candidates. Alex Hazard, for one. He would understand if anyone did; he'd been through a similar situation a year or so ago, with painful results. Laurel, Becky, her other women friends. Mom and Dad. They'd be supportive, all of them, at least up to a point in her folks' case. And yet she was incapable of taking the first step—an emotional quadriplegic.

She started the car, drove carefully out of the lot. Kumquat Street was only a little more than a mile from the high school. Until recently, in good weather, she walked or bicycled both ways; every day now she drove. The car was security, a means of protection against vulnerability. A steel-and-leather cocoon.

The house was big, old, gingerbready, with a wraparound front porch and two massive tulip trees on each side—part of her inheritance from Grandmother Tolliver, and the reason she and Burt had moved up here from the city after their marriage. One of the reasons. The other was the offer from the school board to teach English grammar and American literature at Los Alegres High.

She put the car away in the garage, sifted quickly through the mail on her way into the house. Bills and junk. The red light was blinking on the answering machine in the kitchen. No message, just a hang-up—another damn telemarketing call, probably. She went into her office, switched on her computer, checked her e-mail. Spam.

Five days now Burt had been gone on his latest business trip. And she'd heard nothing from him, not a word.

And for the past six weeks—

Distant, uncommunicative.

Late, very late, coming home from the office two and three nights a week. Working, he'd claimed, but she'd called West Coast Suppliers four times, and no one had answered.

More "business trips" than usual.

Gone from her even when he was home. Their lovemaking had dropped from several times a week to not at all, Burt offering this or that excuse when she tried to entice him.

The conclusion was obvious. Obvious and trite and wrenching. Who?

The owl voice again, echoing in her mind. Who? Who? Somebody she knew, one of their friends? That would be the hardest to take. Laurel? Ridiculous. Becky? Of course not. Ann? Janet? No. It had to be either a casual acquaintance or a stranger.

A bar pickup, in the city or on one of his legitimate business trips? That would be almost as bad as a woman she knew—some boozy tramp with a bag of bed tricks and a full complement of AIDS potential. Least likely possibility. Burt didn't drink much, had never been the pub-crawling type or the kind of man who was attracted to flashy women with low IQs and high-speed libidos. He'd always been a homebody, more inclined to be stimulated by intelligent conversation than a pair of D-cup boobs.

A business associate, then. Someone in his office, or someone he'd met in Kansas City or Chicago or one of the other cities his sales job took him to. Someone bright as well as attractive. Younger, prettier, sexier, smarter than she? A better listener, a more interesting conversationalist? What was it exactly that had attracted him, the quality she didn't have, the thing he must need that she couldn't give him?

She'd always felt they were compatible in every way that mattered. Intellectual equals. More shared interests than most married couples. Open lines of communication. Enthusiastic sex partners, never denying each other anything in bed. And she was the same woman he'd pronounced beautiful after they met at the Palace of Fine Arts four years ago, even though she knew it was more flattery than fact. She hadn't gained an ounce, had no gray hairs, wrinkles, age lines yet. Only thirty-four and still sexy enough to provoke appreciative looks, even a leer now and then, from her male students.

Then what had driven him to another woman? Boredom, a sudden urge for excitement? An early midlife crisis? Just to find out if sex was better with someone new?

Four years. She'd been so certain she knew all his flaws and weaknesses. Moody sometimes, a little stuffy, a little too cool and unflappable. Not conservative enough in his handling of financial matters, particularly when it came to the stock market; he'd made more than one bad investment in recent months, including a pair of Nasdaq fliers that had eaten up most of the remaining cash Grandmother Tolliver had left. Unyielding on what he referred to as "the kid issue," the only thing other than money that they fought about. But unfaithful? She'd have sworn he would never stoop to so much as a one-night stand.

The house seemed too quiet, too empty, as it always did when Burt was away—now more so than ever. She boiled water for tea, took the steeping pot and a cup along with her briefcase onto the enclosed side porch. She opened a window for ventilation, sat at the wicker table, and emptied the case.

Term papers, mostly, from her senior American Literature classes. Early hand-ins from the better students; the rest would come in on deadline next week. Less than a month until the end of another school year. Until summer. The past three years summer had meant travel, more time for reading, more time with Burt. Tentative plans for a trip to Acapulco in August, but those were on hold now along with everything else.

She poured tea, busied herself with the essays. Choose an author from the selected reading list, and a work by that author not covered in the class curriculum. Discuss the work, its relevance among the author's other writings, and its influence (if any) on American literature, using specific examples from the text to illustrate your points. Relatively simple assignment that called for a certain amount of creative thought and writing. Fairly predictable choices so far: Melville's *Typee,* Twain's *Connecticut Yankee in King Arthur's Court,* London's *Smoke Bellew,* Hemingway's *Old Man and the Sea.* The one unusual selection was Steinbeck's *In Dubious Battle.* She picked that one to read first.

It was well done, comparing the novel's prolabor theme with that of *The Grapes of Wrath* and two other 1930s proletariat novels. But she kept bogging down in it, losing the thread; the words seemed to blur together into a meaningless jumble. When she found herself rereading the same paragraph for the third time without comprehending its meaning, she gave up. Try again later, force herself to concentrate—she couldn't afford to fall any farther behind than she already had.

She poured tea, drank tea, stared out at the white fleshy blossoms of the tulip tree.

Who?

Why?

It was the questions, the not knowing, that was intolerable. She'd confront him when he got back, demand the truth. She didn't want to lose him—the prospect terrified her—but she was damned if she'd turn into a Tepid Tolliver, a deaf-and-dumb doormat wife, to keep him. No matter what happened, she could not let it go on like this.

Jessie

Santa Fe, New Mexico

LUNCH at the Shed, dinner at Atalaya. And no pass from Frank when he escorted her back to La Fonda. He suggested a visit to the Puye cliff dwellings next morning, and she said yes without hesitation. Why not? He was pleasant company; he had a storehouse of amusing anecdotes, he seemed interested in what she had to say, he made her feel comfortable in an uncomfortable role. It had been a long while since she'd been involved in the dating game, not since she'd met Darrin a year after graduating from Swarthmore, but she hadn't forgotten the ground rules or the subtle maneuverings, the way one move led to another. The role-playing had been amusing and exciting when she was twenty, but for a widow nearing forty that sort of thing struck her as superficial and predictable and unsatisfying—no longer a game but a tedious, faintly silly ritual. With Frank Court, she didn't have to indulge in it. At least not so far.

The trip to Puye provided her first real uplift of spirit since Darrin's death. Ancient petroglyphs, cavate rooms, and ceremonial kivas carved from soft tuff bedrock, spectacular views from the Pajarito Plateau above—there was something about moving among the ruins of lives lived more than five hundred years in the past that diminished your troubles, gave you perspective on your own life, on life itself. At Puye, in an odd and comforting way, Darrin seemed not quite so completely lost to her, and she felt less alone. She took several photographs to commemorate the visit. Frank had a camera as well and insisted on snapping her in various poses, but he wouldn't let her reciprocate. Camera-shy, he said.

Afterward, there was a picnic lunch at a roadside stream. And a drive through the broken buttes and sage-dotted flatlands of the Santa Clara Pueblo. And drinks and dinner at another of Santa Fe's premier restaurants, the Petroglyph. And at the hotel elevators later, a brief good-night kiss that was more chaste than anything else.

The following evening was Dalishar's party. Frank had asked her to spend that day with him, too, on a round of the gallerias, but she'd declined—as much to test his reaction as for any other reason. Fine. No pressure, no sulkiness or other warning sign of the control freak. Oh, he was aggressive enough, a little full of himself at times, a man used to getting his own way, but those were flaws she could put up with if they were kept within reasonable limits. And he had so many good qualities to counterbalance the flaws: intelligent, broad range of interests, well-developed sense of humor, solicitous without being fawning, and such a good listener that she found herself telling him more than she'd have thought herself capable about her and Darrin and their life together.

Dalishar's home was a walled hacienda in the low foothills off the old Santa Fe Trail, an attractive place on at least an acre of ground. The man himself turned out to be less appealing. Piercing light blue eyes, longish dark hair, and a sculpted, wiry beard that gave him a faintly Satanic look. He was gracious enough, but with an aloofness in his manner that was offputting. An egotist, the kind of man who believed himself to be several notches above his fellow human beings. That was evident in the faintly condescending way he spoke to guests, and the ostentatious display throughout the house of dozens of his paintings, all with the same weird, disturbing quality of *Devil's Wind*, full of demons and witches and hobgoblins. One, of what she took to be the Grim Reaper except that the figure had the head and beak of a vulture, was so repulsive she couldn't look at it for more than a few seconds.

Nor did Jessie much care for Dalishar's girlfriend. Serena, no last name, was at least fifteen years younger than his forty or so— the slinky, vampirish type (powdery skin, jet black hair and outfit, blood-red lipstick and nails)—and neither very bright nor very sophisticated. She was another egotist, given to announcing that she was a crystal and quartz sculptor who intended to be "famous some day." A substance abuser, too, judging from the dilated brightness of her eyes.

The night was warm, and the thirty or so guests congregated in a lantern-lit central courtyard. There was a full bar, a buffet table, even a strolling flamenco guitarist. Not Jessie's milieu, but she'd done her share of socializing with Darrin in Philadelphia and New York, and Frank's presence and a glass of chardonnay made it easy enough to mingle. He seemed to know most of the guests, and he was the sort who would be at ease in any social situation.

The atmosphere and the conversation were stimulating. She established a rapport with a Native American silversmith named Mira Ortiz who shared her views on a number of subjects, and indulged in a spirited political discussion with a conservative couple from Albuquerque. The good gay feeling, aided by the wine, stirred other feelings too long tamped down and ignored. She felt closer to Frank, more attracted to him. Once she caught herself looking at him in the glow of one of the hanging lanterns and wondering what he would be like in bed. The thought vanished as quickly as it had come, yet it left a residue of excitement.

The party broke up before midnight. On the drive back to La Fonda she kept telling herself to go slow; it was foolish to rush into a sexual relationship with a man she'd known less than three days. Darrin . . . but Darrin was gone, and she was still here. Besides which, she knew he'd approve. Love was one thing, sex was another; there was no disrespect in satisfying a biological need. If he were the survivor, he wouldn't have waited seven months to do it.

The inner tingling had grown into a command by the time they reached the elevators. Without any more thought, she took Frank's hand, drew him into one of the cars, and pressed the button for her floor. He smiled at her, but he didn't speak; neither did she. She let her mind go blank, let the hunger take over.

He was every bit as accomplished a lover as she'd imagined— slow-handed, undemanding, paying as much attention to her pleasure as to his own. Long, gentle coupling, without urgency, its peak reached easily and mutually, its descent gliding. Her release was nowhere near as intense or satisfying as the orgasms she'd shared with Darrin, but in a significant way it was their equal because it marked the end of her limbo of grief and loneliness, the reemergence of self. Afterward she lay quiet in the warm darkness, Frank's head on her breast, her fingers stroking that beautiful mane of his. And for the first time since Darrin's death, she knew peace again.

She had begun to drowse when Frank's voice, muffled against her flesh, drifted up to her. "Jessie? Sweet?"

"Mmm?"

"I have to say this—I'm in love with you."

The drowsiness fled. "Oh, now. One night in bed . . ."

"It's not just sex. It's you, everything about you."

"We hardly know each other."

"That doesn't matter. Not to me. I know myself, trust my feelings. I understand if you don't feel the same way yet, and the last thing I want to do is pressure you, but . . ." His lips moved over her still-swollen nipple. "You're going to think I'm crazy."

"I already think that." She didn't know what else to say.

"I want to spend the rest of my life with you."

". . . You don't mean that."

"I do mean it, sweet. More than I've ever meant anything."

"Now, maybe, after we've made love . . ."

"Now, tomorrow, next week, next month."

"Frank, it's so soon . . . you're not seriously proposing to me?"

"Yes, I am," he said. "That's exactly what I'm doing. I'm asking you to be my wife."

Sarah

Vancouver, British Columbia

A NOTHER cold, wet morning. The rainy season was usually over by now, but not this year. Day after day after day of gray skies, rain, drizzle, fog, howling winds off the Georgia Strait and down from the high country.

Sunday morning. Hangover morning. Dry mouth, dull headache, jangly nerves, chilled on the outside and empty on the inside like a skin of frost around a husk. There were good days and bad days, and this was one of the bad ones. When she felt sixty instead of thirty-six. When she was just a pale shadow of the tough-minded, self-sufficient woman she'd always considered herself to be.

Mornings like this, she hated herself.

Mornings like this, she even hated Scott.

Rain ticked and slithered on the window glass. Her flat was on the top floor; she could hear the monotonous dripping beat on the building's roof. She was surrounded by rain and grayness, inside and out—a thought that made her feel even colder. She wore pajamas, socks, a sweater, there was an extra blanket on the bed, the heat was up over seventy. Yet she'd woken up cold, and not even burrowing had taken away the chill.

Sundays were the worst days. Saturday nights and Sundays. During the week and all day Saturday she had the bookshop, twelve to fourteen hours of steady mind-dulling work, and shopping and chores afterward, and then enough Scotch to help her sleep. Saturday nights, though, she couldn't bear the flat alone; so she went out with the few friends she still saw, enjoyed herself once in a while, used alcohol to maintain the pretense that she was enjoying herself the other times. Like last night—lots of Scotch and lots of pretense. And on Sunday she had to hunt for ways to fill the long hours, manufacture outings and mind-occupiers and Scotch-avoiders so she wouldn't be hung over again on Monday. She was at the point now where she was ready to keep the shop open seven days. She'd tried that before, but the location wasn't central enough to Gastown to make Sundays profitable even when tourism was at a peak, and it spread the make-work too thin over the rest of the week. Still, it was better than this.

She wished she hadn't come home last night. She wished she'd gone with David to his big, overheated place in West Van. He'd asked her when they left the Yale Hotel, the liquor making him bold, and she had been on the verge of saying yes. Only then, with the word poised on her tongue, Scott had come crawling into her mind. As usual. And that was the end of that. She'd couldn't get around him to David, drunk or sober, no matter how hard she tried.

In the four years since his disappearance, she'd managed to squeeze past his image just three times. The first Christmas after the accident, when her grief had been so acute she'd thought seriously of suicide, and had taken out the little automatic Scott had bought her and taught her how to use, and been sitting there with it in her hand when David stopped by unexpectedly to bring her a gift; if she hadn't let him stay with her that night, she might actually have summoned enough courage, or enough cowardice, to turn the weapon on herself. The second time, two winters ago on the skiing trip to Whistler/Bascomb; the third time, last summer after the party at David's house. None of the times had been any good for her, though she'd pretended to him for the sake of his feelings. The only thing she had gotten out of them was closeness, connection, warmth.

Trapped in an intimate, impossible relationship with a ghost.

She turned her head. The ghost's framed photograph smiled distantly at her from the nightstand. She slid a hand from beneath the covers, drew the frame to her, and propped it on her chest. It was the only likeness she had of Scott, a candid shot taken on the

Harlans' boat in Victoria Harbor one summer afternoon. He hadn't realized he was being snapped, or he'd probably have protested; that quirky aversion of his to cameras—"Photos are just frozen pieces of the past, and I prefer to live in the present." It was a full-body shot, in three-quarters profile, head back and chin up, a far-away look in his eyes and his wonderful hair windblown. Typical pose. The way she preferred to remember him.

The ache started again; she returned the photograph to the nightstand. Her arm was coated with gooseflesh. Abruptly she swung out of bed, went into the bathroom, and turned on the shower. By the time the water heated, she was trembling. She stood under the steaming spray for a long time, the water as hot as she could stand it, until the shaking stopped and most of the chill was gone. But inside there was no warmth, and before she finished toweling dry, her skin began to pucker and turn icy again.

Quickly she dressed as before, burrowed into bed. The long day stretched out ahead of her; she forced herself not to think about it. Concentrate on being warm, think warm thoughts. One of the beaches on Maui or southern California, blistering hot sun beating down . . .

The phone rang. David or Gwen Harlan—they were the only friends who continued to call on Sundays. She almost didn't answer it because it meant getting out of bed again. But the insistent jangling went on and on, like a prod on her nerves. Finally, in self-defense, she threw the bedclothes back and went out into the living room to put an end to the noise.

David. His rumbly voice said, "Morning. I didn't wake you, did I?" with his usual cheerfulness.

"No. You know I never sleep late on Sundays."

"How's the head?"

"Fine," she lied.

"I wish I could say the same for mine. How about letting me treat you to a little hair of the dog—brunch and champagne cocktails at Hotel Vancouver or the Pan Pacific?"

"I don't think so, David. I don't feel like dressing and going out."

"Cocooning day?"

"The weather being what it is, yes."

"Well, I could drive over and cocoon with you."

"I wouldn't be very good company."

"You sound down. Never a good time to be alone."

"I'm all right. I just . . . I can't seem to get warm."

"Damn rain. Spring's late this year."

She was shivering again. She pulled the robe more tightly around her, and when she did that, her eye fell on the lithograph in the corner alcove, Goya's *Madhouse,* with its twisted, silently screaming faces. She hated it, the terrible agony it evoked, but because it had been a gift from Scott, she'd never been able to bring herself to hide it away in a closet. Now, as she looked across at it, gooseflesh crawled on her arms again, on the outside of her thighs. An involuntary shudder clicked her front teeth together—a sound like bones rattling.

"David?"

"Still here, love."

Sarah closed her eyes. Surprisingly, Scott's image didn't materialize. Away haunting someone else this morning?

"I've changed my mind," she said. "If you'd like to come by . . ."

"You know I would. How about on the way I pick up a video and some beer and a pizza?"

"I don't feel like beer. Or pizza. A video, though . . . something funny."

"Right. Noon, one o'clock?"

"Now would be better."

"Now?"

"Unless you have something else that needs doing."

"Not a thing." She could hear the hope in his voice again; the hope and the hunger and the quiet desperation. "At your service."

"I'll leave the front door unlocked. Don't bother to ring, just come on in."

"Where will you be?"

"In bed."

Sarah could hear the catch in his breath before he said, "Thirty minutes."

She hurried to the front door to take off the locks, then half ran to the bedroom and crawled back beneath the covers. She lay there watching the rain on the window, listening to it beat down on the roof, her body so cold it might have been wrapped in ice packs, her mind a willful blank—a barrier to keep Scott's ghost from creeping in.

Waiting for David to come and make her warm, if only for a little while.

Morgan

Los Alegres, California

SOMETHING woke her from a fitful doze. Burt? No . . . just the damn wind, blowing hard now, clattering something in the empty night. Shadows beyond the windows jumped and danced in the moonlit living room.

She was on the couch, cramped into one corner with her legs drawn up. Her left arm, jammed against the armrest, had gone to sleep. She eased into a sitting position, feeling logy, a dull ache in her temples. What time was it? She peered across at the luminous digits on the VCR. One-thirty? No, 1:20.

One-twenty A.M. Friday morning already.

And Burt still hadn't come back. After ten days of utter silence, the longest he'd ever been away, he'd finally returned Wednesday evening. Been briefly attentive, then cool and distant, refusing to explain either the length of the trip or his silence. Stayed home less than twelve hours, then left again Thursday noon without a word. And no sign of him since.

She rubbed her arm until a pins-and-needles tingling replaced the numbness. Outside, the wind slammed against the house, lashed the branches of the tulip trees into a frenzy. She hated high winds; they made her skin feel tight and sensitive, frayed her nerves, as if she were being sanded inside and out. At night, especially—the way the wind played with the shadows, threw goblin shapes across the walls. All the sounds it made. Stadium sounds: shouts, shrieks, whoops, swelling boos and cheers. Hurt sounds: whimpers, moans, little shuddery cries. Lonely sounds. Dying sounds.

The wind drove her off the couch; thirst took her into the kitchen. Without putting on the light, she crossed to the sink and twice filled and emptied a tumbler. Her head continued to ache. She thought of taking three or four aspirin and going to bed. But that would be giving in, breaking the pact she'd made with herself earlier. No more days and nights like this one. She hadn't quite been able to confront him when he came back from his trip, if he'd even gone on a trip, but when he returned this time, she could and would. Not in bed, though. Not lying down.

Who?

Why?

Tonight, tomorrow, whenever he came home again. And when she had the answers, she'd tell him, "Her or me, you can't have both of us," and make him decide then and there.

Back to the living room. She put on a lamp to chase away the shadows, found the remote, and clicked the TV on to drown out some of the wind sounds. Images flickered on the screen, people running in the woods to the accompaniment of weird percussive music—running aimlessly in straight lines and zigzags, the way it looked, round and round like dogs trying to catch their tails. Like her the past two months. Scared and fleeing emotionally from the unseen and unknown.

"Emotionalism in women is a sign of weakness, abjectness, and/or deep-seated rage." The old Germaine Greer argument, parroted by Mom and Dad in one form or another—one of the reasons she'd never been able to confide in them. If she'd told them about Burt, one or both would have said, "Be calm, take control of the situation." Yes, all right. That much she agreed with. But then one or the other would surely have said, "Make an appointment with a marriage counselor and convince Burt to go with you." Germaine Greer metamorphosed into Dear Abby. Counseling was not some sort of magic panacea guaranteed to cure every stricken marriage, any more than emotionalism was a debilitating disease. Turning her problems over to a stranger did not constitute taking control of the situation; and turning herself inside out, trading deep feeling for cool pragmatism, would not automatically make her a better, stronger, less angry person. You had to work with what you had, within the framework of your makeup and your beliefs. That was the only rational way to handle any crisis.

The figures on the TV screen were still running, but now there were gunshots and screams and hammering drumrolls . . . sound and fury. She pushed the mute button on the remote. Even the wind's racket was preferable.

She sat staring at the flickering images, trying not to think anymore. Might as well try not to breathe. It was warm in the room . . . too warm. Her palms had an itchy feel, as if the skin were cracked and flaking.

One-thirty-nine by the VCR clock.

At 1:57, the wind in a momentary lull, she heard the sound of Burt's BMW turning into the driveway. She sat up straight on the couch, knees pressed tightly together, as headlight glare flashed across the curtained front window. All right. Just remember to stay calm. Two rational adults here. She switched off the TV and waited stiffly.

He came in through the front door, bringing a cold draft with him. The latch clicked, the security chain rattled; then she heard him walk toward the living room doorway, drawn by the lamplight.

He stopped when he saw her. "Oh," he said, "you're still up."

"Waiting for you. We have to talk, Burt."

"It's late, and I'm tired."

"Right now. Here, not upstairs."

He hesitated, then moved slowly to his chair and lowered himself into it. "Well?"

"Yes. Well. Look at me, Burt."

He looked at her. After a few seconds he said without inflection, "How long have you known?"

"Did you really think I wouldn't figure it out?"

"I thought maybe, just long enough . . ."

"Long enough for what?"

"Never mind. I should've been more careful, I suppose."

Careful. My God, careful! Sitting there relaxed, no expression on his face, no remorse or guilt in his eyes or voice. Mr. Cool. Wavy hair neatly combed, tie neatly knotted, all scrubbed and polished and innocent-looking with those mild brown eyes and that handsome face. As if it weren't almost two o'clock in the morning, and he hadn't just come from another woman's bed and body.

Evenly she asked, "Who is she?"

"Does it really matter?"

"It matters to me. What's her name?"

"I won't tell you."

"She's someone I know, is that it?"

"No."

"Do you love her?"

"In my way."

"What does that mean, 'in my way'?"

"Just what I said."

"Do you still love me?"

"In my way."

"Stop saying that! Do you or don't you?"

"Love is different things to different people, Morgan."

"Oh, for God's sake. That's trite, and you know it."

"It's still true. I'm sorry."

"For what? Being trite? Cheating on me with another woman?"

"Sorry it has to be this way."

"What way?"

"Confrontational. I was hoping to avoid that kind of thing."

The wind was at it again, shrieking, gurgling, chuckling. Maniac sounds. They matched a kind of rising wildness in herself, as if she too might start gibbering any second.

"I don't know you," she said. "Four years, all we've shared, and you're a stranger to me."

No response.

"I know, that's trite. Trite and true. Do you think you know me? Or am I a stranger to you too?"

"No one knows anyone, not even himself."

"Another trite-and-truism. We're really on a roll tonight. Is she the first, whoever this bitch is?"

"She's not a bitch."

"No? Does she know you're married?"

No response.

"If she does, then she's a bitch." The bitterness kept leaking out in spite of her vows to remain calm and in control. "How many others, Burt?"

"Would it make you feel better if I said none?"

"Is that a yes or a no?"

"No. Not while we've been married."

"Then why this woman? What's so special about her?"

"I can't answer that. Why does any man fall in love with any woman? Why did you fall in love with me?"

"Oh, bullshit," Morgan said. "Is she young, smart, sexy? Big tits? Suck your dick better than I do?"

The words seemed to shock him. "Stop it. That's beneath you."

"Nothing's beneath me, the way I feel right now." But he was right. She was starting to lose it. If she gave in to her baser emotions, let herself turn into a screaming harpy, she wouldn't be able to cope with the aftermath; she'd close off, shut down, fall apart. She took a breath before she said, "You can't have both of us," in a strained voice. "You must know that."

"I know it."

"Well? Which of us is it going to be?"

No response.

"I'll put it another way," she said. "Are you going to stop seeing her?"

"No. I can't."

"Why can't you?"

"It's time."

"Time? Time for what?"

No response.

"For God's sake. I don't know what you're saying to me."

"I'm sorry."

"Sorry, sorry! Burt . . . if you care at all about me, about saving this marriage, you have to end it with her. Right away. If you don't—"

"Don't threaten me."

"I'm not, I'm trying to—"

He surprised her by getting to his feet in that amazingly quick way of his—seated one instant, standing the next. Surprised her further by saying, "I'd better go now."

"Go? Where?"

"Upstairs to pack a few things. I'll pick up the rest tomorrow or Sunday."

Oh, my God! "You're going to her? Just like that?"

No response.

"You don't have to leave—"

"Yes I do. This is your house, after all." He punctuated that with a strange little unreadable smile, swung around, and left her there staring after him.

Her control slipped again. Desperation filled her. She hated him in that moment more than she'd ever hated anyone—and yet the thought of losing him to a nameless, faceless woman was unbearable.

She ran upstairs after him. He was already in their bedroom, at the walk-in closet, bent over and pawing among the luggage at the rear; straightening and turning with his black leather overnight case in one hand.

"Burt, don't *do* this."

"You haven't left me any choice."

"*I* haven't left you—!"

"Let's be adults about this, Morgan," he said. "No more angry recriminations. This is difficult enough as it is, and nothing you can say will change my mind. It's too late now. It's over."

She moved across to the bed, slowly, not quite steadily. Sat on the edge and watched him put things into the case with his usual methodical care. Underwear, socks, two laundered shirts, one of his Gucci ties. Watched him go into the bathroom, a short while later emerge again with his shaving kit and toothbrush, and add those to the bag. Watched him take his charcoal gray suit out of the closet, the one she'd never liked.

"You don't look good in dark gray," she heard herself say numbly. "You never have. It's wrong for your coloring."

He came over to stand in front of her. The odd little smile was on his mouth again.

"If you're thinking of touching me," she said, "don't do it. I couldn't stand it."

"I wasn't going to touch you. I only want to say—"

"No more 'sorry.'"

"—that I wish it didn't have to end like this. I truly do. If it'd been up to me, I would have avoided this sort of unpleasantness."

Go to hell, she thought. But she couldn't say the words.

"I'll call before I come back for the rest of my things. So you won't have to see me again." He picked up the case. At the doorway he stopped and turned briefly, just long enough to say, "Good-bye, sweet. I'll miss you—I mean that." And then he was gone.

Sweet. That goddamn pet name. Like she was a piece of candy, not a wife, a woman, a human being. Old, stale candy that he'd just spit out.

She wanted to jump up, chase after him again. She wanted to understand how this could happen, why her life was all of a sudden being turned upside down. She wanted to be held, comforted. She wanted to break something—break him, trade pain for pain.

She sat there.

Listening to the sounds of his car starting up, backing out, going away. Listening to the wind moaning and crying in the night.

Jessie

Elton, Pennsylvania

VEN before she returned home, she knew she'd made a mistake with Frank Court. Not the affair itself; she'd needed that, benefited from it in more ways than one. What she regretted was not saying no, gently but firmly, to his astonishing proposal of marriage. Instead, flattered and touched, she'd given in to the closeness of the moment, to her uncertainties and insecurities, and said she'd think it over—foolishly allowed him to believe there could be a future for them. Poor judgment. More than that: an act of cruelty to a man who had treated her decently, and to herself.

The simple truth was, she didn't love him. And she really didn't know him. For all his charm and tenderness, he might well have a dark side. His fascination with macabre art hinted at one. Big rush, constant attention, marriage proposal immediately after their first sexual contact—weren't those all warning signs of the potential abuser? Another: his lovemaking was so intense that it overwhelmed and disconcerted her. Another: his self-assurance bordered on the relentless—a man certain of what he wanted and convinced that sooner or later he would have it. Still, he'd made no demands on her, hadn't attempted to control her in any way, in fact constantly reassured her that he would not try to rush her into a permanent relationship. Hadn't exhibited any signs of violent temper, or even of anger.

It was probable that he was exactly what he appeared to be, a good, sincere man who had met a woman and fallen in love with her. It wasn't unusual; it happened dozens of times every day. The problem, aside from the fact that she hadn't fallen in return, was that she was not ready for another "lifetime commitment." (A term Darrin had used and that she knew now could be a damn hollow lie.) After what she'd shared with Darrin, she wasn't sure she could ever love another man enough to want to spend the rest of her life with him.

They hadn't been two people, she and Darrin, they'd been a single unit, a four-armed, four-legged, two-headed freak. Siamese twins, for God's sake. It was why they hadn't had children, wasn't it? Too selfish to be good parents, and wise enough to realize it and take steps to avoid it. Children would have intruded on, detracted from, their total devotion to each other. She hadn't lost a husband when he suffered his fatal heart attack; she'd lost the other half of herself. And the dessicated remains were still attached, a kind of bittersweet burden she would carry around with her until her own death.

She'd intimated this to Frank in New Mexico, without going into details, and he'd seemed to understand. Fundamentally, he'd said, he was the same type of person—a believer in the single-unit marriage. Well, maybe he was. Maybe he honestly felt he could have that kind of relationship with her. But it was all one-sided. As soon as they were separated, the doubts had crept in; she'd felt no sense of temporary loss, as she had every time Darrin had gone away from her, and no strong yearning to see him again. Actually, in a way that made her feel ashamed, she'd been more relieved than anything else when Frank drove her to Taos and left her there alone.

She hadn't talked to him since, but he'd told her that he would be busy and might not be able to call for a few days. And now that she was home again, she had evidence that his ardor hadn't cooled any. Two dozen long-stemmed red roses were waiting for her, along with a card that read "Welcome home, Darling" and was signed "All my love, Frank."

She'd barely had time to put the roses in a vase when Brenda came knocking at the front door. "I've been home less than five minutes," Jessie said. "You must have radar."

"Brenda Norris, All-Seeing, All-Knowing. Actually, I happened to be out in the side garden when you drove past. How was the trip?"

"A drink first. Then I'll tell you."

"That bad?"

"No, not bad. Interesting . . . too interesting."

"Ah. That must mean you got laid."

Jessie gave her a wry smile. Radar, all right. Brenda knew everybody's business, and what she didn't know, she intuited. If you didn't know her well, you might consider her a busybody; but she was too easygoing, too good-hearted, too willing to lend a sympathetic ear or a helping hand ever to give any real offense. She could annoy you, but not for long. How could you stay annoyed at a Lucille Ball lookalike, complete with henna rinse, who could be as funny as Lucy Ricardo and unrepentantly bawdy besides?

They went into the front parlor, always Jessie's favorite room in this too big, too drafty, old-fashioned colonial farmhouse. She opened the curtains so she could look out over the lawn and garden and Keene's Antique Barn, to the village and rolling hills beyond. Home . . . God, she was glad to be back.

When they were settled with a pair of vodka tonics, she told Brenda about the affair with Frank Court—including, on demand, some of the more intimate details. Brenda, divorced for three years, was currently "between gentlemen friends," as she put it, and her appetite for the salacious was insatiable. But the marriage proposal and Jessie's misgivings put a damper on her enthusiasm.

"Question, for the sake of argument," she said. "Let's say he quit rushing you, backed off, gave you time to get to know him. Any chance you could grow into the relationship, learn to love him?"

"I don't think so. Even under the best of circumstances, long-distance relationships seldom work out."

"Didn't you say he was willing to move back here?"

"Another of his surprises. It wouldn't be a problem for him, he said—the type of freelance work he does, he can live anywhere. But if he actually did move close by, I'd feel even more pressured. More worried, too. What normal man would move twenty-five hundred miles without a definite commitment?"

"The kind who's a fool when it comes to love."

"Men don't have a monopoly on that score," Jessie said rue-fully.

"So all right," Brenda said. "If you're positive you don't want this relationship to go any further, tell him so right away. Don't wait for him to call. Call him."

"I don't have his number. Or his address. There's no listing for him in the San Francisco directory."

"Uh-oh. He didn't volunteer, and you didn't ask."

"It didn't occur to me until it was too late."

"Thinking with the wrong part of your anatomy, Jess."

"Not thinking at all is more like it."

"What about his e-mail address?"

"I don't have that, either."

"But he has yours, I'll bet. And your phone number and home address."

"Yes, as a matter of fact."

"What else did you give him?"

"What else is there? Why, what're you thinking?"

"I'm not thinking anything. Just wondering."

"If he might have some ulterior motive, is that it?"

"Well, you're not exactly without means, as they say."

"Frank doesn't know that. We never discussed my financial status."

"Some men can smell money as easily as they can smell pussy."

"Oh, Brenda, come on. It's *me* he's interested in, and that's not a conceit."

"I still say chalk him up to experience and get rid of him quick, in no uncertain terms. Tonight, if he calls."

Jessie sighed through a mouthful of vodka tonic. "He'll call. He'll want to know if I got home all right, if I received the flowers."

But he didn't call that night. Or the next day.

She found herself listening for the phone, pouncing on it the few times it rang like a cat on a ball of yarn, wanting to hear the sound of his voice and dreading it at the same time. She checked her e-mail half a dozen times: nothing. It put her in a perpetual state of suspense; she couldn't concentrate on business matters, couldn't seem to settle back into her normal, comfortable routine.

Brenda was philosophical. "Well, he's had as much time to think about the affair as you have. Maybe he decided he wasn't in as much of a hurry to get tied down as he thought he was. He might even have met somebody else."

"Maybe, but I don't believe it."

"That's ego talking."

"No, it isn't. You wouldn't think so if you'd met him, seen us together."

"Okay. So it could be business, something urgent that needed his attention—"

"So urgent he couldn't find a few minutes to pick up a phone?"

"—or, God forbid, he had an accident or . . . something."

Something like a sudden heart attack, she meant. "Whatever the reason," Jessie said, "I've got to talk to him soon. I'm not a passive person, Brenda, you know that. I can't just pretend Santa Fe didn't happen and hope I never hear from him again."

"I know."

"Talk to him and make a clean break, for both our sakes. The way I feel now . . . I'm right back in limbo again."

Sarah

Vancouver, British Columbia

THE call came a few minutes before eight on Friday evening.

She was alone in the bookshop, in the glass-walled cubicle that served as her office, paging once more through the spring-summer publishers' catalogs and making minor alterations on her advance-order sheets. It was make-work, an excuse to stay late; being alone here was always preferable to being alone in her flat. There was an almost pleasant, lulling quality to the shop at night, the lights turned down, the quiet broken only by the faint hum of Gastown traffic outside, the shelves and tables of hardcovers and paperbacks a friendly presence.

She had always loved books—the feel and smell of them as well as what they had to offer between their covers. New, old, fiction, nonfiction . . . it didn't matter. There had been plenty of all kinds in her parents' house, and growing up in a small town in the Okanagan Valley, shy and introspective by nature, she'd spent far more time curled up reading than in any of the usual kids' activities. One of her schoolmates had begun calling her "the book lady," and the name had stuck, a source of mild amusement even to her.

She'd begun writing poetry when she was ten, articles and sketches at twelve, short stories at fifteen. Later efforts were good enough to be published in her school literary magazine and the Weehaugan newspaper. At the University of British Columbia she'd taken a creative writing course; her dour instructor had told her she possessed a "raw, undisciplined minor talent" and offered little encouragement. She'd set out to prove him wrong. For three years she wrote feverishly, producing dozens of works, submitting them to magazines in both Canada and the States. One short story —ironically enough, on the theme of unfulfilled ambition—had been published in a small American literary magazine; one eight-line poem had been accepted by a Toronto poetry journal. That was all.

Disillusion set in near the close of her senior year at UBC, and she stopped writing altogether the summer after graduation. The problem, she'd decided, was that she didn't have enough experience to write well about life and the human condition. So with her father's financial support she'd traveled in Europe, the United Kingdom, the States. She had her first love affair in Edinburgh, with a medical student at the university there. She climbed a mountain in Austria, learned to sail in the Mediterranean and survived the capsizing of a yawl in a sudden storm. She was assaulted and nearly raped in a backwater town in Texas. She filled notebook after notebook with these and other experiences; with observations and long descriptive passages. After two years she'd decided she was ready to start writing again, and returned to British Columbia to begin work on a novel. . . .

She was losing concentration. Fatigue did that sometimes even here, weakened her mental defenses and allowed the past to seep in. She took off her reading glasses, pinched the bridge of her nose, rubbed her eyes. Her vision had begun to worsen, one of the reasons for her frequent headaches. She was long overdue for a glaucoma test and a new, stronger prescription. Long overdue for a physical checkup, too. More than two years since her last gynecological exam, her last mammogram, her last bloodwork. She meant to make appointments, but when the time came to follow through, she found excuses to continue postponing. Dangerous apathy. She was listless, run-down; God knew what else might be happening inside her body, what preventable disease might be incubating.

She looked out across the shop. The front window had misted, making the streetlights beyond look smeary and indistinct. Drizzling again. No sun this week, and more damp weather predicted for the weekend. Gray outside, gray inside. And not even the prospect of David's company to make Saturday night and Sunday tolerable; he was away in Calgary on a legal matter and wouldn't be back until late Sunday.

Sarah put her glasses back on, opened another catalog. The print seemed as foggy as the lights outside the front window. She made an effort to bring the page into dull focus. Oh, fine, lovely. The listing she was looking at was for one of those self-indulgent books international best-selling writers seemed fond of perpetrating, a combination of autobiography and how-to-write-and-become-as-famous-as-I-am. She'd read a couple of that type out of curiosity; what they said, when you distilled all the verbiage, was that writing and selling were really pretty easy for anybody who applied himself, and fame and fortune were less the result of luck and heavy financial backing from publishers than of honing one's talent in established patterns. Which was bullshit of the most offensive sort.

Bitterly she remembered the novel she'd labored over for eighteen months after her return to Weehaugan, and the dismissive refusals from four literary agents, the two lukewarm rejection letters from fiction editors in London and New York, the printed slips from a dozen others. And the fresh and consuming disillusionment that had followed. When the Bright Lights Bookshop came up for sale and her father offered to buy it for her, she'd abandoned her dream and slipped sideways into bookselling. Her true calling, she supposed, like it or not. During the early, happy years with Scott, her creative juices had stirred a bit and she'd written a couple of short stories and a handful of poems, but strictly for her own amusement; Scott was the only one who had read them, the only one who ever would. Over the past four years . . . not a word. Nor was there ever likely to be again.

The short, tragic life of Sarah Danner Collins. Not much of a life, really, when you looked at it objectively. A few high points, a whole wriggling nest of failures, disappointments, compromises, tragedies—first her father's fatal aneurism, then Scott's inexplicable accident—and lonely, leaden days. Sometimes she felt as though her life was already over, as if she had died without even knowing it and was nothing more than a reanimated corpse going through a daily routine of programmed actions and responses.

Her head was aching again. Brainstrain, eyestrain, nothing to eat all day except two pieces of toast for breakfast and a sandwich for lunch. She went to the bathroom, swallowed four aspirin. What she really wanted was a drink, two drinks, enough Scotch to let her sleep, but the aspirin would have to do for now. She splashed her face with cold water. It was while she was drying off that the telephone rang.

Her first thought was that it was a wrong number. Customers and acquaintances seldom rang the store after hours, even when they knew she was here. She returned to her office, not hurrying, and was at her desk when the answering machine clicked in and played her recorded voice.

Then she heard, "Pick up, Mrs. Collins. I know you're there." Male voice, a kind of subtenor and unfamiliar. Pause, and then he said, "It's important. Pick up," in a tone that was more command than request.

She caught up the receiver. "Yes, who is this, please?"

"My name doesn't matter. My business does."

"It's after hours—"

"Not the book business. Far from it."

"I don't understand."

"You will. I have something you're going to want to buy."

Now she was irritated. "Is this some sort of telemarketing call? If it is—"

"It isn't." He laughed, a piercing noise that made her wince. "What I have to sell is personal. Strictly between you and me. Something you'll want badly enough to pay a lot of money for."

"What do you mean, a lot of money?"

"Five thousand dollars."

"Five thou—! You must be crazy."

"Like a fox. That's five thousand American, not Canadian."

"What could you possibly have that would be worth that much to me?"

"Information you can't get anywhere else."

"This is a ridiculous conversation," she said. "Either come right out and say what you mean, or I'm going to hang up."

"I wouldn't do that. You'll regret it if you do."

"Are you threatening me?"

"I don't make threats. I sell valuable information."

"For God's sake! Information about what?"

"About your husband."

". . . What did you say?"

"You heard me. Your husband, Scott. You thought he died four years ago, but he didn't. He's alive, Mrs. Collins."

The words froze her in place. Literally froze her; she couldn't move, couldn't speak.

"He's alive," the voice said again, "and for five thousand American dollars, I'll tell you where you can find him."

Morgan

Los Alegres, California

FRIDAY was a lost day. She couldn't face school and called in sick; couldn't get out of bed at all except to use the bathroom. Mostly she slept from dawn to dusk, and got up then only because she was dehydrated and her body craved nourishment. Two glasses of orange juice, half a piece of bread that gagged her, and back into the darkness of the bedroom.

Burt didn't call, didn't return to the house. Punishing her even more? She didn't know, could not seem to come to terms with any of it. Their middle-of-the-night scene seemed long ago and far away, not quite real, as if it were something she'd imagined or lived through in a drugged state. Like the one time she'd experimented with hashish in college—a slowed-down, remote, slightly distorted block of nontime that had left her unable to separate the real from the illusory.

Defense mechanism, that and all the sleeping. The person you loved telling you he no longer wanted you, without warning or compassion, then walking out as abruptly as though you'd been together four days instead of four years. Refusing to name the other woman. Saying words that seemed foreign and inexplicable, as though he'd lost command of the English language or she'd lost the ability to comprehend it.

Saturday morning, after another twelve hours of fitful sleep, she felt better. Clearheaded, more in control. At first she tried telling herself that if he didn't care about her, she was better off without him; but the lie was too great to swallow whole. Then she tried to tell herself that maybe he'd change his mind, come back and beg her forgiveness. If he came crawling, she'd make him suffer for a time, but eventually she'd take him back, no use kidding herself. Only that kind of happy ending was no easier to swallow than the lie. He wouldn't come crawling, not Burt. He was a man who would never crawl for anyone.

The marriage was over.

Accepting that was the first step in getting through the crisis. Accept it, adapt to it, move on. Too emotional for her own good, yes, but no matter what her parents or Germaine Greer believed, she was not weak. She could be beaten down, but she wouldn't stay beaten; her survival instincts were too strong. The only danger was in relying too completely on herself, shutting everyone else out while she rebuilt her defenses. Leading a more or less normal life was an important part of the healing process. Alex Hazard had managed it after his wife left him for another man, hadn't he? Take a lesson from him.

She had no appetite, but lack of food had made her light-headed. She brewed coffee, poured juice, scrambled eggs, buttered toast. By an effort of will she got most of it down, sitting at the table by the big windows that overlooked the back lawn and garden. Birds chattered at the feeder out there; she could hear the distant buzz of a neighbor's power mower. Familiar, ordinary—the illusion of normalcy. Exactly what she needed right now. It looked like it was going to be a warm day, maybe later she'd go for a walk—

The phone.

Her stomach clenched; her pulse rate jumped. Burt?

The ringing went on and on. The answering machine must be off—she hadn't thought to switch it on. The noise seemed as abrasive as fingernails on slate. When she couldn't stand it any longer, she sucked in her breath and snatched up the receiver.

"Ah, there you are. I didn't interrupt anything, did I?"

Laurel. Relief and disappointment, in equal measures. "No, I was just . . . doing some chores."

"With or without that husband of yours?"

"Without. He's not here."

"You're not a golf widow today, too? Men, good Lord, what's so damn appealing about whacking a little ball around a lot of bumpy lawn?"

"I don't know where Burt is," Morgan said. "He . . . left early, while I was still asleep."

"Really?"

"Yes, really. What's so strange about that?"

Too fast, too defensive: Laurel picked up on the tension in her voice. "Something wrong over there? You sound edgy."

Everything's wrong over here. Listen and I'll spew out the whole sad, bitter, miserable story so I can stop choking on it. But all she could say was, "No, nothing's wrong. Just feeling blah."

"Period?"

"Yes," she lied, and went on to butter the lie: "You know how it is the first day or two."

"Don't I just. Women have it lousy, you know that? Sometimes I hate men just for being men. I mean, goddamn it, I really hate the bastards sometimes."

Morgan could find nothing to say to that.

"Oh, hell," Laurel said, "why bitch about something you can't do anything about." Then she said tentatively, "Were you and Burt in Santa Rosa yesterday? Out on the Mark West Springs Road?"

"No. Why do you ask that?"

"Oh, I had a lunch at John Ash, and afterward I went over to the shopping center off Mark West, and as I was leaving I saw Burt. Anyway, I thought it looked like him and his car."

"He was with a woman?"

"Yes, but . . . well, I guess it couldn't have been Burt."

"Why couldn't it?"

"The woman in the car . . . I only had a glimpse, but her hair was shorter and darker than yours. I don't know why I thought it was you. Or Burt. Now that I think about it, I'm sure it wasn't him."

The hesitations and the fast covering meant she was sure it had been Burt.

"So, anyway," Laurel said, "the reason I called, how about a little lunch and a lot of wine at the Mill? I'm in the mood to get sloshed."

"I can't. Not today."

"Sure? We can talk about what swine men are."

"I have to run, Laurel, I'll call you."

Rushed words, rushed hang-up. Now Laurel would wonder even more about the woman with Burt yesterday. But Morgan had run out of lies, evasions, and she was in no frame of mind for chitchat.

She switched on the answering machine. Back at the table, she moved her chair so she would be sitting in warm sunlight. Outside the birds were still milling around the feeder. The Larsons' orange tabby, Mr. Tom, was making his ponderous way across the top of the gated fence that separated this property from Town Creek and the eucalyptus-bordered park beyond; as usual the birds paid no attention to him. Mr. Tom spent a great deal of time on the fence, bird-stalking, but he was old and clumsy and inept and made only halfhearted attempts to snack on a sparrow or robin. As far as Morgan knew, the cat had never even come close to catching one.

Laurel's call had upset her again. She couldn't seem to sit still. The birds, Mr. Tom, the garden . . . none held appeal or distraction. Nor did housework, schoolwork. Or reading. Or staring at the tube. Or shopping or going for a drive—leaving the house at all. She paced the kitchen, the living room. Or pacing. Or even climbing a wall.

Damn you, Burt.

Who?

The owl voice gave her something to do—drove her down the hall and into his study. His domain in every way, furnished to his taste in furniture and art. She seldom went in there, by tacit agreement and because she didn't really feel comfortable in the room. For one thing, the original painting he'd brought home from one of his trips two years ago and hung behind his desk gave her the willies; it was called *The Devouring* and depicted what appeared to be a bunch of ghouls feeding in a graveyard. Burt knew she respected his privacy, would never suspect her of prying among his effects, so it was possible he'd been confident enough and arrogant enough to leave something revealing here. After last night, prowling and prying had become her prerogative.

She couldn't access his e-mail files; he had a security lock on his computer, and she had no idea of the password. But she spent the better part of half an hour hunting through his orderly desk, his meticulous records. No unfamiliar address or phone number, no unusual correspondence or canceled checks or bills or credit card receipts—not a single clue to the woman's identity or where she lived or to any home or business in the Mark West Springs area.

But she did find one thing that puzzled her. In the hand-carved teak box she'd given him three Christmases ago, among a bunch of odds and ends, was a tiny envelope containing a safe deposit key.

At first she thought it was a key to the box they shared at Wells Fargo; it seemed identical to the one on her key ring. Then she looked more closely at the attached brass tag and saw that the number was different. Theirs was 2729, this one 6302. Same type of key, same type of tag and stamping . . . same branch? There was only one in Los Alegres. But why would Burt have rented a second box, at this branch or any other? He could have put anything he didn't want her to see into their joint box; she almost never used it, couldn't remember the last time she had.

She started to replace the key; her name wasn't on 6302, she couldn't get into it. Or could she? Maybe . . . there might be a way. At least she could try. She went upstairs, slipped the key onto her key ring. What time was it? Almost one o'clock already—too late to get to the bank today. She'd have to wait until Monday morning. If Burt came back before then and noticed it was missing, she would say she didn't know what had happened to it. Deceit for deceit, with no qualms at all. That was what situations like this did to you.

The thought bred disgust, but it didn't stop her from making a careful search of his half of the closet. She hunted through every article of clothing that hadn't just come back from the cleaner's, even felt inside shoes and shoeboxes. The only item that gave her pause was the .32 caliber revolver he'd insisted they keep in the house for protection. Insisted she learn how to use it, too: two long, unpleasant afternoons at a shooting range, bang bang bang.

Bang.

She looked at the gun with revulsion, shoved it back into the box where he'd stored it, and closed the closet door. Then she rummaged through his dresser drawers, examined the contents of his jewelry case for unfamiliar cufflinks or rings or tie tacks. Nothing there, either.

Downstairs again. His golf clubs were in the hall closet; she lifted each of the clubs from the bag, emptied the pockets, turned the bag upside down. She searched the rest of the closet—coats, jackets, boxes, the dusty back corners of shelves and floor.

Nothing.

By this time she had worked herself into a kind of controlled frenzy. She combed all the other closets, drawers, cabinets, cupboards—every nook and cranny she could think of. Out to the garage, then, to pore over his workbench, hunt through the storage cabinets. And up the ladder to the loft. And down the ladder and out to the gardening shed. She was on her knees, clawing into a bag of fertilizer, breathing in ragged pants, when the rational part of her mind rebelled and jarred her into an awareness of exactly what she was doing.

Crazy. Oh, God, crazy woman down on all fours trying to find evidence of infidelity in a sack of shit.

Jessie

Elton, Pennsylvania

S ERENA, the woman in Santa Fe with no last name, didn't know who Jessie was. Or pretended not to. "What'd you say your name was again?"

"Jessie Keene. We met at the party last week."

"Which party was that?"

"Dalishar's party. Your party. I came with Frank Court."

"Uh-huh, well." The woman sounded vague, more than a little spacey. As if she might be on something even though it was only ten A.M. out there. "Dalishar gives a lot of parties. We meet a lot of people."

"Frank wouldn't happen to be there, would he?"

"Frank? Frank Court?"

"Yes," Jessie said, "Frank Court."

"I don't know where he is. San Francisco, maybe."

"Is that where he lives, in the city?"

"Don't you know?"

"I wouldn't be asking if I did."

"I don't know, either."

"Do you have his home phone number, any number where I can reach him?"

Silence. Then, "Who'd you say you were?"

For God's sake! "I'm a friend of Frank's. A close friend. As a matter of fact, he asked me to marry him."

Silence.

"Serena?"

"Really? Frank did?"

"Yes, Frank did."

"So why're you calling here? Tell us the news?"

"I told you, I'm trying to locate him, and I thought you—"

"Well, he's not here."

Jessie ground her back teeth. Slowly, spacing the words as you would with a not very bright child, she said, "Frank and I haven't known each other very long. I don't have his address or a phone number where I can reach him. Could you please look them up for me?"

"You're going to marry him, and you don't know?"

"I am not going to marry him. That's why I need to talk to him—"

"Why not? What's wrong with Frank?"

"I don't love him."

"No? He's pretty cool."

"Please, Serena. Frank's address or just a phone number."

"I don't know what they are."

"You can look them up, can't you?"

"Look them up where?"

Steady, she thought, don't lose your temper. "An address book, a Rolodex, a computer file . . . wherever you keep addresses."

"I don't know where we keep them. Dalishar takes care of all that stuff."

"Is Dalishar home? Could you put him on?"

"He isn't here."

"Where can I reach him? At the gallery?"

"You mean Hazelrigg's?"

"Yes, Hazelrigg's."

"He's not there. I think he's in San Francisco."

"You think? Don't you know?"

"He's full of secrets. Shit, too, sometimes."

"Where does he stay when he's in San Francisco? A hotel?"

"No, he doesn't like hotels."

"An apartment? A house? With Frank?"

"He took me with him once. We stayed at somebody's house."

"Frank's house?"

"No. Frank wasn't there."

"Who was there? Whose house was it?"

"I don't remember."

"*Where* was it? What part of the city?"

"I don't know San Francisco, I've only been there a couple of times."

"Near downtown? Can you remember any landmarks?"

"Near the ocean, I think. You could walk over to the beach."

"Ocean Beach?"

Giggle. "Some beach with the ocean right there. Must be Ocean Beach, right?"

"When he's in San Francisco," Jessie said, and her voice sounded strained and a little desperate in her own ears, "when Dalishar is in San Francisco, is there a gallery he goes to? One that exhibits his paintings?"

"I guess so. He's pretty famous, Dalishar is."

"What's the name of the gallery?"

"Which gallery?"

"The one in San Francisco that exhibits his paintings."

"I dunno. Just a gallery."

"He never took you there? Never mentioned it?"

"Duncan? Hey, I just remembered that name."

"The Duncan Gallery?"

"Duncan, that's all. You better ask Dalishar."

Deep breath. "I'd rather ask Frank. Do you know what company he works for?"

"Who, Frank?"

"Yes. Frank."

"Some computer company. That's what he says."

"Computers, yes. He must have mentioned the name—"

"I don't think so," Serena said. Now she sounded bored as well as stoned. "Listen, I have to pee. What'd you say your name was again? Joanie?"

"Jessie. Jessie Keene. If Dalishar calls, would you please ask him to—"

"Fuck Dalishar," Serena said. Then she said, running the words together, "I really have to pee why don't you marry Frank he's a good guy" and broke the connection.

Jessie put the receiver down, thinking sardonically that if she needed another reason not to continue the relationship with Frank Court, she'd just talked to it. Dalishar had struck her as odd, but Serena was downright strange—Vampira on the outside, space alien on the inside. Made you wonder if all of Frank's friends were so far out of the mainstream. If *he* was, beneath his normal exterior.

She called directory assistance in Santa Fe again, this time for the number of the Hazelrigg Gallery. The woman who answered couldn't or wouldn't confirm that a Duncan gallery in San Francisco—"I'm not familiar with the name," she said—handled Dalishar's weird paintings. Wouldn't give out any other information, either. She kept saying, "I'm sorry, I'm afraid I can't help you," as if a programmed loop had kicked in.

Another call to directory assistance in San Francisco. No listing for any art gallery with Duncan in the name.

One more possibility: Mira Ortiz, the Native American silversmith she'd met at Dalishar's party. But there was no listing under that name, in Santa Fe or any of the nearby communities.

Dead end. She couldn't remember the names of the Albuquerque couple she'd discussed politics with, or the other friends of Dalishar's she'd met that night. Too many people, too much wine and body heat.

Darrin's image smiled up at her from the frame she kept on her desk. And his voice seemed to echo in her mind, that amused tone he'd used when he thought she was being stubborn or silly or both.

Let's analyze this, shall we? Are you really worried about Frank Court? Or is it just that you don't like the idea of being unceremoniously dumped?

Of course I'm concerned.

Be honest, now. You want to be the dumper, not the dumpee.

What I want is a clean break. Civilized and final.

Why? You got what you needed in New Mexico, now you're off the hook. Quit chasing after him.

I'm not chasing after him. I want to know why a man tells me he loves me, asks me to marry him, sends expensive flowers to welcome me home, and then suddenly drops out of my life.

Keeping you in suspense. A ploy to make you say yes to his proposal.

I don't think so. He's not like that.

How do you know? You don't know a bloody thing about him, except that he's good in the sack. Not as good as me, but—

Shut up.

So what is it that's really worrying you? That something isn't quite kosher about Frank and his friend Dalishar?

All right, dammit. Yes.

And not knowing what it is, what kind of man you've gotten mixed up with, has you just a little scared, right?

Jessie said aloud, "I'm not going there, I am *not*," and willed her mind blank.

She left the house and walked down the driveway to the big, old, red-painted barn she and Darrin had converted into Keene's Antiques. No cars were parked on the gravel lot in front, but there had already been one customer this morning. When she entered, her assistant, Maude Tyree, announced with a broad smile, "Believe it or not, I just sold the Belter table. Not five minutes ago."

Jessie was surprised. It was a piece that had gone begging for more than five years, a massive rococo table made of black walnut with exaggeratedly scrolled contours, curved legs, and an intricately carved naturalistic motif of roses, grapes, leaves, and birds. Too ornate for most modern tastes, but in good condition and a prime example of the work of the Victorian New York craftsman John Belter.

She said, "Not for the full asking price?"

"Yes! They didn't even try to haggle. They're having it picked up and shipped on Monday." Maude rolled her eyes and added, "Main Liners, of course."

People who lived in Philadelphia's exclusive Main Line, she meant. The kind of people Jessie knew all too well: rich, pampered, sheltered, and inclined to look down their noses at anyone who wasn't in Dun & Bradstreet or couldn't trace their lineage back to pre-Revolutionary days. Darrin's family had been Main Liners, and they hadn't approved of him marrying a New Jersey girl with no pedigree—her parents, owners of a small office supply business, and her upbringing were strictly middle class, and her B.A. degree was from Swarthmore rather than Vassar or Wellesley or Bryn Mawr. If his people had known before the marriage that there was Jewish blood in her ancestry, they would have had fits. She'd told Darrin, of course, and it hadn't mattered a bit to him. She remembered, smiling, that he'd taken a certain perverse delight in informing his father of the fact on their first wedding anniversary. To his father's dying day, he had never again been more than barely civil to her.

Maude thought the smile was because of the sale. She said, "Don't you just love 'em? Main Liners with more money than sense or taste?"

"I can think of another descriptive noun," Jessie said. "I'm going out for a while, but I should be back before noon. Want me to pick up a sandwich for you from Rosen's?"

"If you don't mind, thanks. Turkey on rye. And a pickle." Maude reached under the counter for her purse.

"No, no, this one is on the Main Liners."

It was a warmish day, and Jessie walked the quarter mile into the village. Elton's business district, if you could call it that, was only two blocks long and picturesque without being tricked up for the tourist trade. Fields and rolling, wooded hills surrounded it— "a perfect place to live," Darrin had said when they first came here. Yes, and a perfect place to die, too.

She sighed and went on through the village to the last building on the south end, Fox Earth Gallery, so named as a form of mild protest: Brenda hated the sport of foxhunting that had once thrived in Bucks County. If anyone could find out about Dalishar's background, and where his paintings were exhibited in San Francisco, it would be Brenda.

Sarah

Vancouver, British Columbia

SCOTT was alive.

A miracle, an answered prayer. *If* she could believe the voice on the phone.

Demanding payment for accurate information was cold but understandable behavior; blatant extortion was cruel, monstrous. Except that she wasn't a likely target for that kind of swindle. Not wealthy, just a struggling bookshop owner. And even at the time of Scott's disappearance, the incident hadn't been unusual enough to attract much media attention. The only way the phone call made sense was if this man, whoever he was, had chanced on the knowledge somehow and determined to take financial advantage.

She believed—she refused not to believe. It *had* to be true.

Scott was alive.

Yet other doubts lingered to torment her. If he was alive, why hadn't he contacted her? What had happened on the Island four years ago; how had he survived the accident? Where had he been since, and where was he now?

She imagined him lying in a hospital somewhere, in a coma. Or physically well but suffering from amnesia. Head injury, wandering around all this time with no knowledge of who he was . . . did things like that happen outside of bad TV movies? There must be some other explanation.

Here's one: He didn't want to come home.

No.

He disappeared on purpose.

Crazy notion. Why would he do such a thing?

Problems in their marriage, no denying that. Strain on both sides during the last few months. Suppose he'd gotten fed up, decided a sudden disappearance was preferable to a messy divorce. . . .

He wasn't like that, he wouldn't hurt her that way.

Then what had happened at Tofino? Why hadn't he come home?

The man on the phone had the answers, but the answers were five thousand dollars away, and she didn't have five thousand dollars; she didn't have five hundred dollars. She was sure she could get it, she'd told the voice Friday night, but it would take a little time—Monday at the earliest. He'd agreed to wait until then.

David. Who else but David? It would be painful to ask him, to beg him if necessary, but there was no other option. She would do anything to find out where Scott was.

She had tried to reach David in Calgary, but she didn't know where he was staying, and he wasn't checked in at any of the big hotels, and each of the times she tried his cell phone number, it was out of service. She left messages on his home and office voice mails: Please call me as soon as you get this—urgent. And then she waited in an agony of hope, doubt, confusion. Friday night, Saturday, most of Sunday . . . sleepless nights, interminable days.

David still hadn't returned or contacted her when the stranger called her at home late Sunday morning. And this time he'd been angry when she told him she was still trying to raise the money. "You've got until tomorrow night," he'd said. "After that, the price goes up. A thousand for every day you keep me waiting."

The afternoon crawled away. She couldn't work, couldn't do anything except hide in her flat and will the phone to ring. By the time David finally called, at a few minutes past four Sunday afternoon, she was so stressed she could barely talk.

David's house in West Van was a testament to the success of his law practice. It was on the rocky shore of Burrard Inlet, in an affluent neighborhood of private homes and high-rise condos—an angular modern pile of glass, wood, and stone, shaded by cypress and pine and partially hidden from Marine Drive by a stone fence overgrown with huge rhododendrons. He lived there alone, tended to by a woman who came in three times a week to clean and prepare meals. "I don't know why I bought the place," he'd said to Sarah once. "Status, I suppose. I rattle around in it. What it needs is what I need, somebody to share all that space."

Meaning her. Meaning: Marry me, move to West Van, share my house and my ketch and my membership at the Hollyburn Sailing Club and the rest of my upscale lifestyle. Let me take care of you. Let me love you, even if you don't love me. Poor David. They were two of a kind, each pining away for somebody they couldn't have. For the past four years they'd shared that kind of misery. Now . . .

Sarah turned off the Drive, between the stone pillars and under the arch above the curving driveway. He must have been watching for her arrival; even before she shut off the engine, he was out of the side entrance and hurrying toward her. Big man, broad across the shoulders, thick through the waist, square-faced, his sandy hair thinning on top. Not handsome, not even very attractive—not her type at all. And yet there was something about him that comforted her, made her feel safe when she was with him. His size, maybe. His calm intelligence. The fact that he was always gentle with her, as if she were an object of great fragility.

She let him embrace her. When she drew back, he maintained his hold on her arms while his eyes searched her face. She'd calmed down after his call, washed her face and put on makeup before leaving the shop, but the ravages of the past three days showed through. He said, "My God, Sarah, you look . . . exhausted. Are you all right?"

"Yes. Just not sleeping well."

"You sounded pretty upset on the phone. What's happened?"

"Can we talk inside?"

"Of course."

He took her arm, led her into the house to the massive living room at the rear. The outer wall was entirely glass, the curtains open to reveal, beyond the clifftop terrace, a sweeping view of Howe Sound, Bowen Island, part of the spine of Vancouver Island in the far distance, the spires of the Coast Range to the north.

Cloud-filtered sunlight glinted off the water, off the hulls of tankers and freighters anchored in the narrows—the first sun they'd seen in what seemed like weeks. An omen?

David sat her down, gently, on the couch. "Scotch?"

"Please. But make it a small one."

He poured two fingers of Glenlivet for her, a double for himself. It wasn't his first; she'd smelled it on his breath outside. When he handed her her glass, she saw the lines and shadows in his face, the deep fleshy sacs under his eyes. "You look tired yourself," she said.

"Long damn stay in Calgary."

"You work too hard, David."

"And you don't? Just a couple of workaholics, that's us."

And we both know the reason why, don't we? she thought. She sighed and sipped Scotch, girding herself.

"Now tell me what's got you so worked up," he said.

"I need to ask a favor. A big favor."

"Name it."

"I wish I didn't have to, I swore I'd never ask anyone for—"

He waved that away. "Just name it."

"A loan. A cash loan."

"No problem. How much?"

"Five thousand dollars. American equivalent."

If he was surprised, he didn't show it. His only reaction was to lift his glass and swallow a mouthful of whisky. "That's a lot of money."

"I know. I wouldn't ask if I didn't need it so badly—"

"Of course you wouldn't. Just tell me what you need it for."

She had her lie all ready. She hated lying, to anyone and least of all to someone she cared about; it made her feel like a Judas. But she couldn't tell David the truth. Lawyer-fashion, he would try to talk her out of paying the money, insist on other options that would take too much time. She couldn't bear delays or arguments, anything that would keep the man on the phone from revealing his information any sooner.

"I'm drowning in bills," she said. At least that part of the lie had some basis in fact. "That's why I haven't been sleeping. Business has been off, I'm on credit hold with distributors and publishers both, I haven't been able to pay the rent the past two months . . .

I'm afraid I'll lose the shop if I keep trying to struggle along the way I have been."

"This damn economy," David said. "Is five thousand American all you need to get current?"

"Yes."

"You're sure? I can let you have more."

"Just five thousand."

"It's yours. I'll have the money transferred to your account tomorrow."

"Immediate transfer? I mean, so it'll be available right away?"

"Yes. I'll call my bank first thing in the morning. All I'll need is your account number."

"David, I don't know how to thank you—"

"Then don't try. I'd do anything for you, you know that. All you ever have to do is ask."

When she left him a short while later, the feeling of relief was tempered by self-disgust. Such a shabby, manipulative way to treat a friend and nominal lover. He hadn't asked anything in return, even refused—against his principles, surely—to bother with a legal loan agreement; pay him back when she could, he said, her word was good enough for him. Nor had he tried to take advantage of the situation by suggesting or even hinting at bed. If he had, what would she have done? Better not think about it. She felt enough like a whore as it was.

Think about something else.

Think about Scott, alive.

Monday, May 19

Morgan

Los Alegres, California

ONDAY morning. And still no word from Burt.

She called in sick again to the school, then dressed and put on makeup to hide some of the haggard lines and drove downtown. She was waiting at the door when Wells Fargo opened at nine. Alice Kim, she saw with relief, was behind the window that serviced the safe deposit boxes. She'd met Alice at a PTA function two years ago, become friendly enough with her to have been invited to her home a couple of times; her daughter was in Morgan's senior English class.

At the window she forced herself to smile through the usual banal pleasantries and manufactured another half-truth to explain why she wasn't teaching today. She put her and Burt's joint box number on the slip, signed it, and watched as Alice went through the motions of checking it against the file card. Bank routine, nothing more; she barely glanced at the card before she buzzed Morgan through.

In the vault Alice took her key and opened number 2729. "Need a booth?"

"No. Not necessary."

Alice dutifully turned her back while Morgan pretended to slip something inside the box, then closed and locked the drawer again. As they started away Morgan said, as casually as she could, "Oh, I almost forgot—I need something from our other box."

"You have a second?" Friendly question, without curiosity.

"My husband's idea. One of anything is never enough." She extended the key she'd found in Burt's desk. "You know how men are."

"Do I ever." Alice hesitated, but only fractionally; then she accepted the key and turned back along the row of boxes, rounded a corner, and stopped again. Number 6302 was one of the large lower boxes, and when she bent to slide it out, she had to tug on it and then strain a bit to lift it.

"Heavy," she said as she put it into Morgan's hands.

"Gold bars. We're hoarding them."

Alice laughed. "Need a booth this time?"

"Yes, thanks, I'd better."

"I'll be out front when you're ready."

When she was alone she carried the heavy box to one of the booths, made sure the curtain was tightly drawn behind her. Her pulse rate had accelerated; the blood-throb in her ears seemed almost percussive. She leaned against the counter, staring at the gray metal container, afraid now. Pandora's box. Open it, and nothing will ever be the same again.

But nothing would ever be the same again anyway, would it, no matter what she did? And she had to know. She had a *right* to know.

She steeled herself, and raised the lid.

And stood rigidly, staring, unable to move. The screen of her mind went blank, as if a Shut Down command key had been pressed. The word "God!" crawled out of her mouth in a stunned whisper.

Money.

Packets of cash, each fastened with a rubber band, in layers that filled the box top to bottom, side to side.

Eventually her hands moved, without conscious volition. She watched them lift one packet, flip through it, set it down. Another. Another. Another. Some of the bills were new, most were old and well used. A few stacks of fifties, many more of hundreds. At least two dozen packets altogether, each inches thick.

How much?

Fifty thousand?

I hate to tell you this, Morgan . . . severe setbacks in our Nasdaq holdings . . . we've lost almost everything . . .

More than fifty thousand?

Can't begin to express how sorry I am . . .

Edges of something else, she saw then, showed at the bottom of the box where she'd removed one complete stack. Papers of some kind, clipped together. A bulky envelope. She clawed out the contents: passports, photographs. The words and images were blurs; her eyes, her attention, refused to focus. Not here. Not here.

She stuffed the papers and photographs into her purse. Leave the money? No. Half the packets of bills fit into the purse, the rest into her coat pockets. She felt as though she were suffocating, as if the cubicle had become a box as small and tight and airless as the metal one before her. But it was another three or four minutes before she called Alice Kim, before she trusted her vocal chords to produce normal-sounding words.

✦

At the bank—stunned. At home, with the packets and papers and photos spread out in evil little piles on the kitchen table—shattered.

Cash total: $64,200.

Rental agreement and rental receipts, made out by a Santa Rosa real estate firm, for a piece of property on Coyote Springs Road. The agreement was dated March of last year, more than a year ago. The renter's name: Burton Cord. The mailing address: a Los Alegres post office box, the number unfamiliar. Coyote Springs Road . . . she had an idea where that was. Somewhere in the country east of Santa Rosa, off Mark West Springs Road.

Passports. Three of them, in three different names: Andrew Coyne, Scott Collins, Burton Cord. The smiling face affixed to each was the same, or almost the same, twenty-something in the first, late thirties in the one she'd known about, the one made out to Burton Cord.

The photos. Two posed, three snapshots, all eight-by-ten, all in color, all of women who appeared to be in their thirties. Women of a similar type: slender, attractive without being striking, fair-skinned, blond hair and blue or gray eyes. Names written in ink on the back of each in Burt's neat, round hand—first names and below them, cities or towns. The next to last one, the familiar one, read "Morgan—Los Alegres, California."

Marriage licenses. Five altogether, issued in four different states and British Columbia, Canada, over the past seventeen years. The man's names: Arthur Corbell, Andrew Coyne, Stephen

Corbett, Scott Collins, Burton Cord. The women's first names matched those on the backs of the photos. The most recent license, dated four years ago, joined Burton Cord and Morgan Elaine Tolliver in holy matrimony.

Divorce decrees. None.

And the most damning of all—a single sheet of paper, the lines on it penned in Burt's unmistakable hand at different times, in different colors of ink:

Doris		
Minneapolis, Minnesota	3/84–5/88	$159,600
Maureen		
Shreveport, Louisiana	5/88–3/92	$92,400
Jane		
Chicago, Illinois	3/92–6/96	$112,000
Sarah		
Vancouver, British Columbia	6/96–4/00	$108,600
Morgan		
Los Alegres, California	4/00–5/04	$97,300
Jessie		
Elton, Pennsylvania	5/04–?	? ? ? ?

Ninety seven thousand, three hundred dollars. The amount he claimed to have lost in the stock market, all of their savings, the last of her inheritance. Siphoned off a little at a time from their joint account. The source of some or all of the cash in the safe-deposit box.

May 2004. Jessie—Elton, Pennsylvania. The answer to Who. The woman in the last of the six photographs, the woman he'd met on one of his trips, the woman he was leaving her for. His next victim.

She hadn't married Burton Cord four years ago; Burton Cord did not exist. She hadn't shared her body and four years of her life with a husband, a lover, but with something else entirely.

Bigamist.

Thief.

Sociopath.

Monster.

Jessie

Elton, Pennsylvania

THE situation just kept getting stranger, more disturbing.

No word from Frank on the weekend or on Monday. And then Brenda stopped by at cocktail time Monday evening with a report about Dalishar.

"He isn't affiliated with any San Francisco gallery," she said. "Never has been. He's had exactly one West Coast show, at a small Beverly Hills gallery four years ago, and it was a bomb."

"But Frank said he divided his time between Santa Fe and San Francisco, that he was well known out there."

"He may divide his time between the two, but it's not because of any prominence in the art world. He has a small local rep in Santa Fe, but according to the people I talked to, it doesn't extend any farther. Not even as far as Albuquerque. His paintings are just too bizarre for most people's taste and comfort."

"Then why did Frank say—"

Brenda shrugged. "Big buildup to impress you."

"He didn't come on like that."

"Different men, different bags of tricks. You know how they are—always looking for a way to get into a lady's knickers."

"It doesn't make sense," Jessie insisted. "That expensive house of Dalishar's, the lavish party, all those people. And his girlfriend, Serena, told me they entertain regularly."

"It's called a front, Jess."

"You need money for that, too."

"Could be he inherited some or has income from another source."

"Doesn't anyone know for sure?"

"Nope. He's something of a mystery, your friend Dalishar. One person in Beverly Hills called him a 'shadowy figure.'"

"Shadowy? What does that mean?"

"She wouldn't elaborate. But no one seems to know much about his background. He showed up in Santa Fe about five years ago, avoids talking about where he's from and what he did before he became an artist. Keeps his private life almost obsessively private."

"That sounds a little ominous."

"Not necessarily," Brenda said. "It could be an image thing. You know, Dalishar, Man of Mystery. More front, like the lavish parties. Not that it's doing him any good, at least not in the art world."

"I'd still like to know where his money comes from. A behind-the-scenes patron, maybe?"

"Well, there was some speculation along those lines. But if so, nobody has any idea who it is. This woman friend of his, Serena, maybe."

"I doubt that."

"Why? She seems to be another little mystery."

"From the way she talks and acts," Jessie said, "she's a druggie and not very bright."

"Bed partner and window dressing?"

"Exactly."

"She's also several years younger than Dalishar, right? How about spoiled, airhead rich kid attracted to older artist and the art scene?"

"Paying all his bills, buying him that house?"

"Happens a lot more than you might think."

"I don't know, it just didn't feel like that kind of relationship."

"You only spent one evening with them."

"Yes, but still . . ."

"Here's another thought," Brenda said. "What if Frank's paying some or all of Dalishar's bills?"

Jessie stared at her. "*Frank?*"

"Well? Why not?"

"For one thing, he doesn't have that kind of money—"

"How do you know? All you know about him is what he told you, and that's not very much."

"If he was Dalishar's patron, why wouldn't he have said so?"

"Privacy factor, maybe. Or some sort of agreement between them."

Jessie stood, went over to poke the fire she'd lit in the big Inglenook. "I suppose it's possible," she said at length, "but I don't think so. His relationship to Dalishar didn't feel like that, any more than Serena's did."

"All right, so what *did* it feel like?"

"I'm not sure. I can't put my finger on it."

"Casual friends? Business associates?"

"Frank said they were friends, that he admired Dalishar's work, that he wished he were an artist himself."

"So?"

She shook her head. "I wish I had some clear idea. Of that, and what Dalishar does in San Francisco—Serena told me that's where he is now—and why I haven't heard from Frank."

"You're driving yourself crazy with this, Jess. Imagining all sorts of unpleasant scenarios, I'll bet."

She had been, still was, but she said, "I can't stand not knowing. Or much more of this . . . limbo. If I don't hear something pretty soon—"

"What? Don't tell me you're thinking about flying out to San Francisco? Or back to Santa Fe?"

"If I have to," Jessie said, "I'll do both. Whatever it takes to find out what this is all about, and put an end to it so I can get on with the rest of my life."

Sarah

Vancouver, British Columbia

S TANLEY Park, six hundred acres of trees and gardens and hiking paths on a peninsula jutting out into Burrard Inlet, was a cold and lonely place at night. She knew all about cold and lonely places; over the past four years she'd become an expert on them. Her flat on Sundays. The city on gray days in the midst of crowds. But here in this one, tonight, there was none of the emptiness and despair that had enfolded her in all the others. What she felt now was tense expectancy, a tingling excitement in no way sexual, yet not unlike that produced by foreplay. Fear, too—tamped-down, low-grade terror.

On the phone the man had told her to pull off onto the main drive onto the parking area at Hallelujah Point and park in the shadows. He'd stressed that—park in the shadows, and make sure the interior dome light is switched off. Nine o'clock, he'd said. Don't be late.

Nine-oh-five now by the radium dial on her wristwatch. He was the one who was late.

Five minutes. Nothing to worry about yet. Don't even think about the time.

From where she sat she had a panoramic view: the lights of the Royal Vancouver Yacht Club, the dark shape of Deadman's Island just off shore, south across the inlet beyond Brockton Point to the lighted high rises downtown. Stunning on a clear night, remote on a dark, cloud-spattered one like this. City full of people, mostly full of life. Cold. Lonely. Like the burial ground on Deadman's, where the last of the Coast Salish were interred.

She stirred, shivered, drew the collar of her coat more tightly around her neck. Told herself again not to think about the time, not to look at her watch. Looked at it in spite of herself.

Nine-oh-nine.

Lights on the drive behind her, but they drifted on past. Involuntarily she reached out to touch the zippered tote bag on the seat beside her. The bundles of bills—American dollars, "don't bring anything but fifties and hundreds"—shifted inside, made a faint crinkling sound. Five thousand dollars. For a few words, a few scraps of information. It wouldn't matter if they were the words she wanted to hear, scraps she could hang onto, but if they weren't . . .

Nine-eleven.

Another set of headlights on the drive, these coming from the direction of the yacht club. For a few seconds she thought the beams would slide past; then the car turned abruptly into the parking area, the glare sweeping across her car. The other braked fifty or sixty yards away, close to the seawall. The lights winked off.

Sarah sat stiffly, her pulse racing. No one got out of the other car. Maybe it wasn't him, might just be kids on a date or somebody stopping briefly to look at the view—

No, it was him. The door opened, just a parting of the darkness to allow a shape, bulky and indistinct in a heavy coat and low-brimmed hat, to rise up out of the interior. Night wind caught the tails of the coat, flapped them outward and upward so that the shape resembled a huge bat as it moved slowly across to her car.

She stopped watching him and stared straight ahead, as she'd been instructed. The door latch clicked; cold air touched her as he opened the door a few inches to satisfy himself that the dome light was off, then a chilly gust as the gap widened. She felt his eyes on her from outside before he slid in quickly, shut the door to trap them together in the cramped darkness.

She waited for him to speak, her hands tight around the wheel. When he didn't, the silence built oppressively. At length she broke it herself. "You're late."

"Never mind that." Same male subtenor, a little raspier in person. Smoker's voice. American, Canadian? She couldn't place the accent. "You bring the cash?"

"On the seat between us."

She heard him lift the bag, zipper it open, paw around inside. "Money has such a nice feel," he said. "The full five thousand?"

"Yes."

"American dollars, right?"

"Yes. Count it if you like."

"I trust you, Mrs. Collins."

"All right. Can I trust *you* now?"

"Absolutely. Quid pro quo, that's my motto."

"Then tell me about my husband."

"Before I do that, let's get one thing straight. We never had this meeting. No money changed hands. If anybody asks you how you found out, you say the information came from an anonymous caller. Understand?"

"Yes."

"You'd better, if you want to keep things friendly between us."

"I said I understand. Now tell me about my husband."

"He's very much alive, like I said on the phone. Living in California."

"Where in California? What town?"

"Small one north of San Francisco. Los Alegres."

"Is he . . . all right?"

"Hale and hearty. He's using the name Burton Cord."

"I don't understand. You mean he thinks he's someone named Cord . . . doesn't remember his past?"

"Oh, I'd say he remembers, all right."

"An alias, then? Why would he do that? Is he in some kind of trouble?"

"If he isn't now, he will be before long."

"Stop talking in riddles! Say what you mean."

"Sure thing, Mrs. Collins. Facts are what you're paying me for, facts are what you'll get. No more—what's the word? Extrapolations?"

"Good," Sarah said. Her throat felt hot and constricted, as if it might close up and gag her on her own words. "What are the facts? What's he doing in this place, this Los Alegres?"

"Pretending to be a traveling salesman. Computer software."

"Pretending?"

"His address is two-nine-seven Kumquat Street. K-u-m-q-u-a-t. Sounds funny, but it's a kind of fruit—"

"I know what a kumquat is. For God's sake—"

"I have his phone number, but you don't need to memorize it. He's listed in the local directory down there." Cloth rustled as he shifted position. "Let's see . . . I guess that's about all."

"No, that's *not* all. What happened four years ago on Vancouver Island? Why is my husband living in California under a different name? How did you find out all this?"

"Can't help you on any of that, I'm afraid. Not covered in the price." The door latch clicked, chill air rushed in again. "Nice doing business with you."

Panic rose in her. She jerked her head around, caught a glimpse of facial hair beneath the low hat brim as she clutched the sleeve of his coat. He pulled away from her, slid out through the open door.

"Wait! Please . . ."

He hesitated, still facing the car. Then, without leaning down, he said in a different tone, one etched with sly humor. "I almost forgot. There is one other thing I can tell you."

"Yes? What is it?"

"The address I gave you, two-nine-seven Kumquat Street— your husband doesn't live there alone. He shares the house with a schoolteacher named Morgan. His wife—married her just about four years ago."

Morgan

Sonoma County, California

ARK West Springs Road ran east from Santa Rosa to Calistoga, at the tip of the Napa Valley, winding through woodland and cattle graze and along the rim of a petrified forest. Once it had been a quiet country road; now it was a commuter route, truck route, tourist route, with five times the traffic. The side roads that branched off in both directions were still relatively deserted, leading to ranches, farms, private estates. Coyote Springs Road was one of these, a narrow blacktop that serpentined across hilly land, in and out of stands of trees, to the northeast.

She drove slowly, mechanically. The changing surroundings registered for a few seconds, vanished from her consciousness as soon as she left them behind. Her mind was empty, a scooped-out gourd. She seemed to have stopped feeling altogether since she'd left home. Horror, hurt, bewilderment, anger—all gone. No emotional connection of any kind.

The address on the rental agreement was 4320. She focused on mailboxes and gate signs; numbers registered long enough to be disregarded. Thirty-five hundred, four thousand, forty-one hundred . . .

Ahead on the left, a thin column of dust trailed upward, forming a line perpendicular to the road. It was being made by a large, dark-colored car, she saw then, speeding along an unpaved driveway partially screened by madrone trees. The driveway belonged to 4320; she read the large black numbers on the fencepost mailbox just as the dark car reached the intersection. It didn't stop there, barely slowed before it slid into a yawing turn in her direction. In reflex she brought her foot down on the brake pedal. The other car straightened, whipped past her as she craned her neck sideways.

Morgan had a blurred impression of the driver behind a dust-streaked side window. She thought it was a man, alone in the car, but she wasn't sure. Her one other impression was that the car was black and unfamiliar.

Slowly she drove ahead to the dirt lane, turned into it through an open gate in a weathered stake fence. A hundred yards of drive-way ended in a wide flat area stubbled with dead brown grass. A small box-frame house, its fenced yard spotted with weeds and thistles, its front porch overgrown with climbing roses, stood on the left. Behind it was a closed garage, and off to the right, some kind of cinder-block outbuilding about half the size of the house. Trees crowded in behind the house and garage, their wind-whipped leaves throwing shifting patterns of sun and shade across the roofs. There was no sign of Burt's black BMW, or of other cars. Nor any sign of life.

She stepped out, hesitated, and reached back inside for her purse. The wind kicked up as she closed the door, made her shiver even though it was a warmish day. Silence lay over the property, broken only by the wind talking and the distant screech of a jay. Pine scent came to her, along with the ticklish odors of dust and dry grass and growing things. The sounds and smells registered briefly and were gone, in the same subliminal fashion as the sur-roundings on the drive up here.

Walking to the house, her legs had a curiously light feel, as if she were moving on currents of air. The porch steps whispered to her. Off-key chimes came and went deep inside. She waited, clutching the purse tight against her breast.

No one opened the door.

There was an adjacent window covered by slatted blinds. Mor-gan stepped over to peer through the up-canted slats. Part of a bare wall, part of a ceiling that bore an old, yellowish damp stain—nothing else. She backed away, turned down off the porch, and fol-lowed a weedy path to the rear.

The garage had a pair of lift-up doors. She tried raising both; neither would budge. On the near side was a smaller door, also locked, and a single window. The glass was grime-streaked, spiderwebbed on the inside. When she put her face close to it, she could make out the shape of a car slotted within. Not Burt's BMW. This one was bigger, either white or beige—another unfamiliar vehicle.

She made her way through the remains of a vegetable garden to the rear of the house. The screen door there was stuck, but when she tugged on it, it rattled open. The paneled door behind it was unlocked. She opened that, listened, started to call out, changed her mind, and walked in quietly instead.

Kitchen. Clean, the countertops and dinette table empty, nothing in the double sink except a finger-marked tumbler. She picked it up, sniffed it. Scotch. The only kind of whiskey Burt, or whatever his real name was, would drink was sour mash bourbon. She set the glass down again, opened each of the cupboards. All were empty except for a small box of bran cereal in one of those over the stove. The refrigerator contained a mostly full quart of V-8 juice, a baggie of carrot and celery pieces, a carton of fat-free milk. None of that was Burt's, either. He liked whole milk, oatmeal; he didn't like raw vegetables. And he wouldn't touch any kind of juice except fresh-squeezed orange or grapefruit.

She went through the other rooms. Front parlor, tiny sewing room, two bedrooms, one bath—all spartanly furnished. The second of the bedrooms and the adjacent bathroom were the only ones that showed signs of occupancy. Silk sheets and a blanket on the bed, a small-size Pendleton shirt and a pair of jeans hanging in the closet; on the only chair, a leather duffel bag containing socks, cotton underwear, a B-cup bra—and nothing to identify the owner. The dresser and nightstand drawers were empty. No personal items of any kind, not even a package of condoms. Soiled towel on the bathroom floor, a jar of face cream, toothbrush, and a tube of toothpaste on the sink. That was all.

The rest of the house was barren, unlived in. Bare mattress on the bed in the other bedroom, empty closet, empty drawers. Undisturbed dust coated the few pieces of tired furniture in the sewing room and most of those in the parlor. A bottle of Johnnie Walker Black Label Scotch, a third full, sat on a table next to a

worn paisley couch; there was nothing else in there to indicate recent habitation.

Somebody was staying here, or had been recently—a woman,
judging from the bra and clothing, and hardly a glamorous one.
Who? The owl voice again. But there wasn't a whisper of Burt. He
didn't seem to eat here, spend much time here, sleep or even screw
here. What *did* he do here?

Morgan paced back through the kitchen, outside, and around
to the front. The cinder-block building had one door, facing the
yard; it was made of thick wood and double-locked with a deadbolt
and a hasp and padlock. She made a full circuit of the building.
Two windows, both of them tightly latched and curtained in heavy
black muslin. That was one odd thing about it; another was that it
had skylights, two of them set side by side toward the rear. At a distance their bubble shapes were just visible above the roof line.

For a time she stood in front of the door, staring at it, seeing it
and then not seeing it. Seeing Burt's face as if it were superim-
posed on the wood—a harlequin's face, twisted into an obscene
leer. Violently she shook her head to drive it away, then turned and
plodded to the car. The key was still in the ignition; she didn't
touch it. Just sat there without moving.

Questions moved across her consciousness, appearing and dis-
appearing like minnows in dark water.

What was inside the sealed building?

Who was the woman staying in the house?

Why had the driver of the dark car left in such a hurry?

Was Burt coming back here?

What am I going to do now?

She couldn't hold on to any of them long enough to sort out
possibilities. Scooped out, bled dry. Her mind simply would not
function in normal channels.

Her nose began to run. The wind, the dust. She snuffled, realized she was still clutching her purse, snapped it open, and
reached inside for a Kleenex.

Touched metal, cold slick metal.

Her fingers closed around the object, lifted it out to where she
could see it.

Gun. The little .32 caliber revolver.

She stared at it. She didn't remember taking it out of the bedroom closet, putting it into her purse, before leaving home. She disliked guns—what had made her do a thing like that?

Nausea struck her all at once. She threw the door open, leaned out, and vomited stringily into the dead grass.

If Burt had been here, if she'd found him here—

My God, what was I going to do?

Tuesday, May 20

Jessie

Elton, Pennsylvania

O N Tuesday morning she awoke feeling listless and depressed, as she often had in the weeks following Darrin's death. It had taken her nearly three months to shake the hopeless feeling that life no longer had any real meaning for her. When she finally emerged from that cocoon of grief, she counted her blessings—Keene's Antiques, her family in Teaneck, her friends and activities here in Bucks County. Until she let Brenda talk her into traipsing off to New Mexico, they'd been enough to sustain her most days. Other days . . . no.

On days like this one, she understood that she needed more than what she had. Not another man, another husband; the affair with Frank had made that clear enough. What she needed was a purpose of some kind, a motivating force more satisfying than selling antiques and going on shopping sprees in Manhattan and visiting relatives and riding airplanes to places she'd never been. Right now, she had one new motivation: finding out the truth about Frank and Dalishar and the whole Santa Fe interlude. It wasn't much, granted, and its frustrations were responsible for this fresh bout of depression, but it was a purpose nonetheless, and she meant what she'd said to Brenda about seeing it through. Little pit bull with a bone, determined to chew it up and swallow it even if she choked on the splinters.

She checked her e-mail first thing. Nothing. Of course . . .
nothing.

She had no appetite. Breakfast was three cups of black coffee,
and the caffeine made her head feel as if electrodes had been im-
planted behind her eyes. She rattled around the big house, doing
mostly unnecessary chores and telling herself—for at least the
tenth time—that she ought to just sell the house and all the rest of
the property except for the section where the antiques barn stood,
and move into a smaller, more manageable place. But she knew
she wouldn't do it. Darrin's home, her home; the last substantial
piece of their life together. Someday, perhaps, when enough time
had passed. But probably not.

Restlessness eventually took her out to the barn. Its cool, dark
mustiness was a refuge; she locked herself in and left the Closed
sign in the door glass. For a time she puttered, rearranging a display of sterling silver serving pieces, and then retreated to her
workshop at the rear. One of her restoration projects was an early-
nineteenth-century weathervane made of copper and modeled in
the round in the image of Gabriel blowing his horn. It was badly
pitted by oxidation, dented and bent from years of mishandling,
but still salvagable.

She was working on it when the phone rang. There was an extension on the wall next to the workbench; the flashing button told
her the call was on the house line. Her immediate thought was
that it might be Frank. She pulled off one of her gloves, picked up
on the third ring.

"Is this . . . I'm calling for Jessie Keene." Woman's voice, flat,
almost monotonal, with an underlay of something that Jessie
couldn't identify.

"Yes, this is she."

"My name is Morgan, Morgan . . . Cord. You don't know me,
I'm calling from California. The man at Elton Realty gave me your
name and number."

"Did you say California?"

"Los Alegres, California." Another pause. "Does that mean anything to you?"

"No. Los Alegres? I've never heard of it."

"It's a small town north of San Francisco."

San Francisco. A premonition stirred in Jessie, bunched the

muscles across her shoulders. She leaned against the workbench, realized she was pressing the receiver tight against her ear, and relaxed her grip.

"Not as small as Elton, though," the woman said, "and a good thing, or I might not have been able to find you."

"What is it you want, Ms. Cord?"

"Mrs. Cord." The voice was still flat, but the underlying emotion was stronger now, recognizable. Hurt. Deep hurt. "Or so I thought until this morning."

"I don't understand."

"Are you married?"

"Why do you ask that?"

"*Are* you?"

"I'm a widow."

"A widow." Pause. "I found your name in some papers. Jessie— Elton, Pennsylvania. The man at the real estate office said you're the only woman named Jessie who lives there. Is that right?"

"Yes, it is. Will you please—"

"Have you met someone recently? A man?"

". . . Yes."

"In Elton?"

"No, on a trip to New Mexico. Santa Fe."

"Does his last name start with the letter C?"

"Court. Frank Court."

"Late thirties, slender, dark wavy hair . . . beautiful hair?"

"Your husband," Jessie said. Now her voice matched Morgan Cord's—flat, monotonal, underlain with a quality of hurt.

"Burton Cord. Except that he's not my husband. I thought he was, but he's not." Audible breath. "You're lucky, Mrs. Keene. A very lucky woman."

"I don't . . . What do you mean?"

"Are you sitting down?" The woman drew a long shuddery breath. "All right. I'll tell you why. . . ."

Sarah

San Francisco, California

ER flight arrived at SFO shortly before noon. U.S. Customs had been dispensed with at Vancouver International, and all she'd bothered to pack was a small carry-on suitcase; she went straight from the gate to the Hertz counter on the lower floor. Forty minutes later she was in a Ford compact, on her way toward the city.

A California map had pinpointed Los Alegres some forty miles north of San Francisco. A California guidebook had told her it was a town of 50,000 located at the terminus of a saltwater estuary and that there was nothing special about it: founded a hundred and fifty years ago, once an agricultural and poultry center, now a combination of upscale bedroom community and haven for writers and artists. Nothing in any of that provided a clue as to why Scott would be living there.

Two-nine-seven Kumquat Street . . . he shares the house with a schoolteacher named Morgan . . . married her just about four years ago . . .

Some form of amnesia?

I'd say he remembers, all right . . .

The only other reasonable possibility beat at her again, as it had ever since Stanley Park last night. That the whole thing had been deliberate. Planned disappearance, manufactured evidence to support it.

Cases like that cropped up now and then; you read about them in the newspaper, saw detailed reports in TV features, and marveled at how devious human beings could be with enough provocation. Almost always there was some strong impetus to make a person feign his own death, something more than just a simple desire for escape from a marriage, a life, that had grown stale and suffocating. Some type of crime, past or present. Fear of being caught and sent to prison. Run, hide, establish a new identity in a new town, a different country.

He's using the name Burton Cord . . . pretending to be a traveling salesman . . .

Scott, a criminal . . . her mind shied away from belief, crawled back toward it again. If he hadn't lost his memory, if he'd married this woman named Morgan, then he was a conscious bigamist. One felony count against him right there.

She'd lived intimately with him for four years, believed she knew him so well, but David had been so damn right: Everyone has a dark side, you never really know anybody, not even yourself most of the time. What did she really know about Scott Collins? He'd always been reticent about his past, his family, even his work. She'd accepted him at face value, the way you do when you fall in love, marry, set up a life together.

And he'd done this to her, left her to wonder and hurt and grieve alone—an act colder, more cruel, than any sort of physical abuse. He must never have loved her, to care so little about her feelings. Yet he'd married her, he'd been gentle and loving for most of their four years together. How could you reconcile two such opposing sides to the same man?

She was nearing San Francisco now. Traffic had thickened, causing a slowdown as the Nineteenth Avenue exit appeared ahead. You had to go through the western end of the city to get to the Golden Gate Bridge; she remembered that from the one time she'd been here, during her two years of wanderlust after college. Traffic lights made progress even slower. Stop-and-go, stop-and-go.

Her nerves frayed even more. Once she crossed the bridge, it should take less than an hour to reach Los Alegres. And no more than a few minutes to ask directions to Kumquat Street and to drive there. But she had to get to the bridge first.

She tried to work out what she would say to Scott when she came face-to-face with him, but all the words and sentences seemed wrong—trite, silly, too angry, too defensive. She gave it up, finally. The dialogue would be painful enough without planning or anticipation. Just get there, get it over with.

And then what?

It was absurd to believe he would leave his new wife, his new life, and come back to her. Even if she wanted him back, and she didn't, she'd be a fool to try to reestablish a relationship with a bigamist and God knew what else. As soon as she returned to Vancouver, she would file for divorce. That much was certain in her mind. What she did about the rest of it depended on him—how he reacted to her, what the nature of his secret was.

Morgan

Los Alegres, California

S HE opened the front door, hurrying—and Alex Hazard was standing there on the porch with one big freckled hand upraised. She would have plowed into him if he hadn't caught and held her. Fright came and went in a rush; she blinked up at him, openmouthed.

"We've got to stop meeting like this," he said.

". . . What?"

"On a perpetual collision course. Before one of us does some damage to the other."

"Oh. I didn't know you were—" Abruptly she stepped back out of his grasp, clutching the tightly packed briefcase against her chest. He glanced at it, but only for a second; his eyes met hers, and she managed to hold the contact. "Why are you here, Alex? What do you want?"

"Checking up on you."

"What?"

"You've missed the last three days of school. And Becky Lowenstein told me she's called three times with no answer."

Becky, yes. She'd let all three calls go on the answering machine. Two others as well, one from her mother in San Diego. Friends, family . . . she couldn't bring herself to have a conversation with any of them, even a brief one. The only person she'd been able to talk to was Jessie Keene, and making that call, baring her soul to a stranger, had been the hardest thing she'd ever done.

"Morgan?"

"I just haven't been feeling well," she said. "The flu or something . . . I don't know."

"Doctor's appointment?"

"What?"

"Where you're going."

"Going?"

"Coat, purse, car keys and briefcase in hand, and in a hurry. Must be going somewhere."

"I . . . the library," she lied. "Some research I need to do."

"I'd be glad to drive you. You look a little shaky."

"What?" *Stop saying that!* "No, I'm all right, I can drive myself."

"I don't mind—"

"But I do!" Too sharp; the words pulled his brows together, put an odd speculative look on his face. She said, "I'm sorry, Alex," making an effort to soften her voice, "I didn't mean to snap at you. I really am all right. Really."

His eyes said he didn't believe it.

She started to step around him, but he stopped her with his hand, gentle but firm on her arm. "Something's wrong, isn't it." It wasn't a question.

"What do you mean, 'wrong'?"

"Look, Morgan, I'm a fairly perceptive guy. I can tell when things aren't right with a friend, someone I care about."

"I told you, I have the flu."

"Maybe you do. But it's more than that."

"No. You don't know me that well."

He said slowly, "Is it Burt?"

She felt herself flinch, started to say "What?" again, bit the word back and kept silent.

"Problems between you and Burt?"

"You have no right to ask that question."

"Maybe not. Where is he?"

I don't know, I don't know, I don't know! "At work, I suppose. Where else would he be at noon on a weekday?"

"I haven't seen him in a while," Alex said. "Neither has anyone else I've talked to. I drive down this street sometimes, and I haven't seen his car lately. I hate to be blunt, but . . . I know the signs as well as anybody, and you've got them all. I can' t help wondering—"

"What signs?"

"—if your marriage is in trouble, if Burt has moved out."

The feeling of wildness rose in her. When she spoke again, the words had a choked sound. "That's none of your business!"

"Morgan, I didn't mean to upset you. In my clumsy way, I'm only trying to help—"

"Then leave me alone!"

She shook off his hand, hurried down the steps and across to the driveway. It took two tries to get the car door open. She threw the briefcase onto the seat, fumbled the key into the ignition, and then backed up too fast, at an off-angle that brought the tires up onto the lawn. Aloud she said, "Shit!" and maneuvered the car back onto the pavement. Alex was still standing on the porch, watching her; she couldn't read his expression at the distance, and that was good, because she did not want to know what it was.

Once she turned the corner, she felt calm again. And ashamed of herself. Another emotional meltdown. Allowing her feelings to rule her actions. Alex had caught her off guard, but that was no excuse. My God, why hadn't she simply told him some of the truth? She'd told Jessie Keene this morning. And Alex suspected part of it anyway. She could have sworn him to secrecy.

She had to make sure this was the last time she lost control. That crazy episode yesterday, taking the gun to the house on Coyote Springs Road in some sort of half-psychotic fugue state, had really scared her. No more of that lunacy. Tight rein from now on, especially when she saw Burt again.

If she saw him again.

Four days since their late-night scene, and not a sign of him. Something very wrong in that. Understandable that he'd want to avoid her and that he wouldn't care much about his clothing and personal belongings, but he damn well cared about the sixty-four thousand dollars and all the incriminating papers in his safe deposit box. It just wasn't in character for him to disappear without cleaning out that box first.

Jessie Keene had had no word from him, either. Uncharacteristic behavior at both ends.

Had something happened to him?

The thought had been in her head for days now, and it must have been in Jessie's, but neither of them had put voice to it. Hinted at it, skirted it, but kept it off the table. In Morgan's case it was a confused issue. She wanted him punished for what he'd done, but in spite of the episode with the gun, she really did not want him injured or worse.

She'd felt calmer after the call. Jessie Keene was a voice of reason, a sensible, intelligent, self-contained woman who had not fallen completely under Burt's spell, who'd her own doubts about him and felt the same about seeing him punished. They'd talked a long time, awkwardly at first, then more easily. Bonded. A woman she'd never laid eyes on except in a photograph, but who had suffered the same man's abuse and who now shared a common goal of ending his vicious game.

Morgan put the car in gear, drove downtown. Her first stop was Kinko's. She transferred the marriage licenses, passports, photos, rental agreement, and list of names and dollar amounts from the briefcase to her purse, and at one of the self-service color machines inside she made copies of all of them. Jessie's suggestion, and a good one. So was her next stop: a different bank, the B of A branch, where she rented a new, large safe deposit box. Alone in a booth, she put the $64,200 in cash and the original documents inside. Evidence that now only she had access to.

She felt better, much better, after that was done. The prospect of home, all the little reminders of Burt and their life together, had no appeal. She felt like driving, but not aimlessly—some place with a purpose.

She found herself heading south on Main Street to the freeway. It wasn't until she took the exit marked San Francisco that she knew where she was going.

Jessie

Santa Fe, New Mexico

NOBODY home at Dalishar's big hillside hacienda. And judging from a couple of rubber-banded newspapers in the driveway, an accumulation of mail in the pole-mounted box next to the patio gate, Serena had vanished along with her boyfriend. Jessie rang the bell three times anyway, then tried the gate latch. Locked tight. Short of scaling the high stucco wall, she was, in Darrin's quaint epigrammatic phrase, S.O.L.

Now what?

She hated being thwarted when she was on a mission; this thwarting made her even angrier than she already was, and even more determined. She hadn't spent eight hours driving to Philadelphia, sitting in a jet, enduring a wobbly crosswind landing at the Albuquerque airport, and then wheeling a rental car up here to be denied. As tired as she was, she was ready and willing to go without sleep for another twenty-four hours if necessary.

Pit bull was an apt phrase for her in this state. Once she had her teeth into a task or a cause, she was loath to let go. She was a good hater, too—Darrin had always said so—and after the phone call this morning, she had a hate on for Frank Court or Burton Cord or whatever his name was as big as any she'd ever known. Any and all feelings she'd had for him had been dissolved in its acid.

That poor woman in California. All the other poor women on

his list of victims—a list she'd been slated for herself. To think that she'd fallen for his line, slept with him, actually considered a long-term relationship with him! It made her feel stupid and gullible and vulnerable; made her mad as hell. She damned well intended to do all she could to put him in prison where he belonged.

Easier relished than accomplished at this point. Going to the authorities was premature. She was pretty sure, and Morgan Cord had agreed with her, that they didn't have enough hard evidence yet. They needed more facts about Frank Court, they needed the identities and cooperation of his other victims, and for their own protection, they needed the advice and counsel of a good attorney.

She'd placed a call to John Dollarhide, Darrin's lawyer and his father's before him. Dollarhide was the most knowledgeable attorney she knew, and she was sure he would be able to recommend an equally reliable investigative firm. His offices were in Philadelphia, and she'd been prepared to drive up there for a conference, but he hadn't been available. Wouldn't be in the office, she was told, until the following day. She had his home number, and she might be able to reach him there this evening, but then again she might not. And that was when she'd decided to fly to New Mexico, see if she could pry any useful information from Dalishar, Serena, or anyone else who knew Frank. Better to be doing something, even if it proved frustrating, than to let another eighteen or twenty hours of her life slip away in empty frustration.

Only now that she was here, Dalishar wasn't, and neither was Serena. Which left her with one other possibility for tonight.

It was after six, and Hazelrigg's and the other downtown galleries would be closed. Or would they? Heavy tourist trade in Santa Fe, and if it wasn't quite the season yet, the time was drawing close and the weather was good. With luck, one or more of the galleries would be open late.

Hazelrigg's was dark, of course, but she found two galleries nearby that were still lighted. The first had nothing for her. The second, within hailing distance of the Palace of Governors, was just about to close, and the fussy little man who met her as she entered seemed reluctant to attend to any more customers. Dalishar? His

lip curled; Dalishar's work—underscoring the word with faint distaste—was handled exclusively by Hazelrigg's, and he knew nothing about the artist. Mira Ortiz? Her name perked him up a notch.
Excellent craftsperson, he said, created some of the finest silver-
and-turquoise jewelry in the area. He'd handled some of her pieces
in the past, but unfortunately he had none at the moment—

"I met Mira ten days ago at one of Dalishar's parties," Jessie
said glibly. "I should have gotten her address and phone number
then, but you know how it is at parties. Neither one is listed, and
now it's urgent that I speak to her again. I'd be very grateful, and I
know Mira will be, too, if you could put me in touch with her."

"Well . . . we don't give out personal information about our
artists."

"Not even if it's to their benefit? A phone number will do."

"I'm sorry, it's our policy."

"What if you made the call?"

". . . Excuse me?"

"On my behalf. That wouldn't be violating store policy, would
it?"

"Well . . . are you planning to purchase something from her?"

"No. My reason for wanting to see her is entirely personal."

He looked dubious.

"If you'll get her on the phone, you can listen to my end of the
conversation. That should convince you I'm not trying to circumvent a commission. My name is Jessie Keene. She'll remember
me—Dalishar's party ten days ago."

He still wasn't quite convinced. So she showed him her bright-
est smile, the one she used on waffling customers at Keene's Antiques, the one that made her eyes luminous and had the hint of a
wink in it.

"If you'll do that for me," she said, "I'll just look around at all
the lovely pieces you have on display. I'm sure I can find something
that strikes my fancy."

Everybody had his price; she'd found his. He produced an answering smile, said, "We do have some very nice Santa Clara and
Ildefonso pottery, right over there on your left," and went away to
make the call.

Sarah

Los Alegres, California

I T was an old house, Victorian style, on a large corner lot. Wrap-around porch, one side glass-enclosed. Tulip trees, well-tended lawn, rhododendron hedges, narrow strips of garden thick with flowering plants.

Déjà vu: It might have been her former house, transplanted from Vancouver to a small town in northern California. Different, of course, and yet essentially the same. Style, lot size, landscaping . . . all similar, all familiar. Had Scott chosen it for that reason? Changed wives, changed countries, but maintained the same kind of comfortable home environment?

Sarah sat rigidly behind the wheel of the rented car, staring across the street at the house. Seeing it now through a film of un-shed tears. All her bitter resolve seemed to have deserted her. Here, now, looking at the house he shared with his schoolteacher, she could not bring herself to get out of the car, cross the street, climb the steps to the porch, ring the bell. She felt incapable of any kind of movement, as if she had been stricken with temporary paralysis.

I can't face him, she thought. Or her, the new wife. Not yet!

She sat and stared, sat and stared. Details of the house and yard slowly began to register. No car in the driveway or at the curb in front. Blinds and curtains on the facing windows closed. Stillness everywhere on the property except for the faint stir of a breeze in the leaves and branches of the tulip trees.

Nobody home.

Of course not. He had a new job, a salesman's job—he might even be out of town, traveling as he'd done so often during their years together. And the new wife taught school. Midafternoon now. It might be hours before either of them came home.

A kind of dull coward's relief moved through her, faded almost immediately. Postponing the inevitable. Like being given a drug to temporarily ward off pain. It would be just as bad, if not worse, later on.

She could not just sit here and wait. Already she could feel herself tightening inside. An hour or two of enforced waiting, in sight of that unfamiliar-familiar house over there, and God only knew what she might do or say. Go away somewhere, anywhere . . . except a place where liquor was sold. No Scotch until afterward, even though the craving for it had started: dry mouth, constricted throat, vague twitching in her palms and fingers. Find a motel. She would be in no shape to drive all the way back to San Francisco tonight, that was certain. She would need a room close by, a place to sleep, a place to hide.

The sense of paralysis had left her. She started the engine, put the car in gear.

There was neither a motel nor a hotel in downtown Los Alegres. She stopped finally at a service station, spoke to an attendant. He directed her to the D Street bridge, then right on Lakeville— new Sheraton on the river next to the marina, he said. "River" meant the tidewater estuary, which terminated in a boat basin beyond an old-fashioned drawbridge; the motel was a mile south, a new-looking complex that sprawled along the muddy bank. The room she was given overlooked the estuary, wider here and chocolate brown in color, dominated by a huge dredger on the far shore. The view, made even bleaker by clouds and running vanguards of fog, matched her mood.

Her head ached: lack of sleep, travel fatigue, tension. She rummaged in her purse, looking for the tin of aspirin. Before she found it, her fingers touched her cell phone; on impulse she took it out, switched it on, and tapped the message button. Two messages. That was as far as the impulse went; she didn't listen to either of them. They would all be from David, worried about her, wondering why he hadn't been able to reach her. She would call him later to ease his mind. But not until after she met and dealt with the Scott crisis. No matter how it played out, she would not open herself up to David until she was back home, face-to-face.

She found the aspirin, swallowed four in the tiny bathroom. Came back and sat on the bed. The nightstand clock read 3:40. It was cold in the room; she stood to turn up the heat. Sat once more and stared at the window-framed, gray-and-chocolate-brown landscape outside.

Alone again. Cold again.

She lay down with the bedspread over her. The room warmed, but her skin remained icy. Random sounds penetrated the walls. She closed her eyes, opened them and looked at the red numerals on the bedside clock, watched them advance with agonizing slowness.

When 4:00 appeared, she got up and put on her coat and gathered her purse and went out and walked to the restaurant-and-lounge. She stopped just inside the entrance to the lounge. It was deserted except for a woman bartender. Along the backbar, bottles gleamed in the half light.

Just one, she thought.

She took a step inside, stood still again. Why lie to herself? It wouldn't be just one; it would be two, three, four. Dutch courage. And when she confronted Scott and his schoolteacher, it would be with liquor on her breath and her mind dulled—the half-drunk abandoned wife, vulnerable and pathetic, a damn cliché.

No.

She turned abruptly, went outside again. Not far from her room she'd noticed a path that led off through reeds and grass along the estuary. A wetlands area inhabited by ducks, other kinds of waterfowl. Cold and alone out there, too, but it was a better, more tolerable kind of lonely than the room or the motel lounge.

Morgan

Los Alegres, California

THERE was no such company as West Coast Suppliers. Not in the Phelan Building downtown and nowhere else in San Francisco or the greater Bay Area. From the Phelan lobby she called the number Burt had given her, and a woman's voice said, "West Coast Suppliers," the same as always. Morgan asked for Burton Cord and the voice said, as always, "I'm sorry, but he isn't available. May I take a message?" Morgan said, "West Coast Suppliers doesn't exist. Burton Cord doesn't exist. This is some kind of answering service, isn't it?" There was a longish pause, and then a soft click, and the line hummed emptily in her ear.

Another lie. Another deception.

Where had he gone, all those mornings he'd left the house with his briefcase? What had he done during the eight or nine or ten hours until he returned home in the evening? And all those business trips . . . where, why, doing what?

The more she found out about the man she had loved and married, the more unreal the past four years seemed to her. As if she had been living in a fantasy world, a kind of perverted Oz or Wonderland in which nothing was what it appeared to be. And now that she had emerged, it was not into the real world again but into a halfway place filled with shadows and misshapen images.

Van Ness Avenue, Lombard Street, the Golden Gate Bridge,

the tunnel and Waldo Grade . . . so familiar and yet overlain with strangeness. The sun was gone; the day had turned gray, an odd filtered, shimmery gray that made everything look as if she were seeing it through a film of water. She stayed in the slow lane, not trusting herself to drive above forty-five. Wind off the bay and slipstream from passing cars buffeted the Toyota; she clenched the wheel more tightly to hold down the sway, keep within her lane.

On the passenger seat, her cell phone remained silent. She imagined it as a living thing, mocking her—a disturbing image that she quickly walled off. It was too early to hear from Jessie Keene, who might not even have arrived in Santa Fe yet. Burt . . . he wouldn't call her on the cell; she could remember only one time when he'd done that, years ago. There was no one else she cared to hear from. And yet its continued silence was somehow maddening.

Commuter traffic started bunching early on 101 North. Not even four o'clock, and it was a stop-and-go crawl from near the Richmond Bridge exit through San Rafael. A virtual parking lot north of Novato, where three lanes became two over the remaining eleven miles to Los Alegres. When, for God's sake, were they going to widen this corridor? More and more people moving into the county every year—if they didn't do something soon, there'd be gridlock one of these days.

It was a quarter to five before she crossed the county line, nearly five when she reached the downtown exit, after five when she finally turned off Kumquat Street into her driveway. Her hands, the back of her neck, her underarms, were moist with sweat. Now that she was home, the drive up from the city began to seem as surreal as the past four years, the whole outing another little trip down the rabbit hole.

She had pulled the car back near the garage, so the rear door to the house was closest. When she was out and walking, her legs had a light, jellied feel; fog-laden wind dried her sweat and created shivers by the time she reached the door. She didn't need her key—it wasn't locked. In her distracted state she must have forgotten to turn the deadbolt.

She hurried inside, across the utility porch. In the kitchen she switched on the light. And then stood still, a sudden prickly sensation on the back of her scalp.

There was someone else in the house.

She sensed it even before she heard the sounds, bangings and thumpings muffled by the walls. One of the downstairs rooms . . . Burt's study?

Burt?

She hadn't noticed his car, but he could have parked it across the street or down the block—she hadn't been paying much attention to her surroundings when she swung into the driveway. So he'd decided to reappear at last. All right. Confront him and be done with it.

More sounds, a loud banging this time as if something had been knocked over. What was he doing? She pushed through the swing door into the hallway, warning herself again to keep her emotions under control. Yes, his study. She went that way, calling out his name.

The noises stopped.

"Burt?"

No answer.

Morgan took another step toward the study, her mouth open to call out again. In that second he came fast through the open doorway to face her. She sucked in her breath; confusion gave way to sudden terror.

He wasn't Burt.

Big, dark, bearded, wild-eyed—a stranger.

She pivoted, tried to run away from him. He caught her in the archway to the living room; powerful fingers bit into her shoulders, spun her around. A scream rose in her throat. He saw it coming, held her with one hand and clapped the other over her mouth and nose to strangle the cry. Her terror mushroomed. She struggled frantically, didn't have the strength to break free as he pushed her into the living room.

The backs of her legs bumped into something yielding . . . the near end of the couch. He held her there against it, his face close to hers, his breath coming in hard, hot little pants. "I'm going to take my hand away. Don't scream, don't make me hurt you."

She managed to move her head slightly. The pressure of his hand eased, then was gone. She choked on the first heaving intake of air, coughed, sucked in another lungful.

"Where is he?"

She shook her head, still fighting for breath.

"Where the fuck is he?"

". . . Burt?"

"Burt my ass. Come on, come on, you must have some idea where he is."

"I don't . . . no—" She coughed, swallowed. "I haven't seen or heard from him since last Friday—"

"Don't lie to me."

"I'm not lying. I swear, I—"

"All his stuff's still here, he doesn't think I know what he's up to. He must be coming back."

"I don't know!"

"He's coming back." Statement this time, as if he were trying to convince himself. "Bastard won't get away with screwing me out of my share. You hear from him, you tell him that. Half of it's mine now, and I'm going to get it one way or another."

"Half of . . . what?"

The stranger leaned his face even closer, his mouth almost touching hers—an implacable face, blood-darkened, grotesque. Unreal . . . as unreal as everything else, as the next words that came hurtling out at her.

"The money," he said, "the money, *the five hundred thousand dollars!*"

Jessie

Santa Fe, New Mexico

MIRA Ortiz lived in the Eldorado section of the city—both a long and a short way, she'd said on the phone, from her birthplace in the Santa Clara Pueblo. She was open to a brief visit and questions about Frank Court and Dalishar, "though I really don't know either of them very well." Her directions were explicit; Jessie had no difficulty following them.

Mira's home was a modest mission-style adobe, behind which stood a small outbuilding that was probably her studio. A barking dog that turned out to be a fat Sheltie was at her side when she opened the door. "Shut up, Tewa," she said in cheerful tones, and the dog obeyed immediately. To Jessie she said, "He's like a lot of people—likes to hear himself make noise. Don't worry about him. The only thing he's ever bitten is his own butt."

"You can say the same about a lot of people. Metaphorically, anyway."

Mira laughed. She was in her forties, plump and plain except for waist-length black hair that must have been stunning when she was younger and was still enviable despite its frosting of gray; but when she laughed or smiled, it gave her face a radiant quality that transformed it from plain to attractive. She was aware of the fact because she laughed and smiled often.

They settled in a clerestory-beamed living room, in front of a piñon fire in a kiva-style fireplace. The rough plaster walls and simple furnishings were decorated with a variety of Native American art—woven rugs, black Santa Clara pottery, ceremonial masks. Unlike Dalishar's home, none of her own works were in evidence here. The greater the talent, Jessie thought, the more secure the artist and the less the need for ego-flaunting.

The Sheltie curled up alongside Mira's chair and watched Jessie with solemn eyes. A coal-black cat appeared, conducted a brief examination from a distance, and disappeared again. "Another of my housemates," Mira said. Except for the animals, she lived alone. She'd confided that at Dalishar's party, along with the information that she was divorced and had a daughter who was a premed student at the University of New Mexico.

"So, Jessie," she said then. "What brings you back to Santa Fe so soon?"

"A personal matter. I'd rather not go into the details."

"Then I won't ask for any. But from what you said on the phone, it has to do with Frank Court and Dalishar."

"Frank Court, mainly. I'm trying to locate him."

"He doesn't live in Santa Fe, you know."

"I know. In California, near San Francisco. He . . . hasn't been home in several days."

"Have you talked to Dalishar? I think Frank stays with him when he's in Santa Fe."

"Dalishar's not home, either," Jessie said. "I spoke to his girlfriend long distance yesterday. She said she doesn't know where Frank is. And now she seems to be gone, too. Their house is locked up tight."

"Well, I don't know where they might be. I haven't seen either of them or Frank since the party."

"Can you tell me anything about Frank—his work, his background, other friends in the area?"

"Sorry, no. I barely know him. I've only seen him a few times."

"At Dalishar's?"

"There, and at a couple of gallery openings and an art show. The only things we've talked about is art." Pause. "He's a very charming man."

"Oh, yes," Jessie said. "Charming."

Mira looked at her closely for a few seconds. Her expression said she was beginning to understand the situation. She was wrong, of course; but what she thought she knew seemed to engender sympathy, put her solidly on Jessie's side.

"If he has any other close friends here," she said, "I don't know who they are. He and Dalishar always seemed joined at the hip at social functions."

"What's their relationship exactly? Just friends, or is it more than that?"

"Well, art and the art scene. Other than that, I'm not sure."

"Private people."

"Yes. Very."

"What can you tell me about Dalishar and Serena?"

"Facts or impressions?"

"Either one."

"He's a lousy artist," Mira said. "Conceptually, that is. He has an adequate sense of color and form, but everything he's done has the same dark, brooding, unpleasant quality. And I'm not the only one who thinks so." Her smile was wry this time. "A reflection of his personality."

"That sounds as though you don't much care for him."

"Honestly? I can't stand the man. Or his lady friend."

"But you attend his parties."

"I attend a lot of parties. A lot of openings and shows." Pointedly she added, "So do art patrons and gallery owners."

"I understand his paintings don't command large sums."

"Hardly. If he's sold one for as much as a thousand dollars, I'd be amazed."

"Then how can he afford the lifestyle he leads?"

"Good question. One I can't answer."

"Serena?"

"You mean does she come from a wealthy family? I doubt it. She's not well educated and not very bright—more interested in what she can put up her nose than the junk she creates out of crystal and quartz. My daughter met her once. Her opinion is that Serena is part witch woman and part turtle."

"Turtle?"

"Hard shell and easy to put on her back." Mira laughed.

"Is there anyone locally who might be paying Dalishar's bills?"

"No. If he had a local patron, I'd know it or at least have some idea. If he has a patron at all, it's somebody in San Francisco. A woman, probably."

"Why San Francisco? And why a woman?"

"He spends a lot of time out there. At one of his parties I overheard him mention a woman who lives in the city—another artist, someone he seemed to have known for a long time." Pause. "Come to think of it, it was Frank he was talking to."

"Did he say the woman's name?"

"Not that I recall."

"Did she have anything to do with a gallery in San Francisco?"

"That wasn't the impression I got, no."

"Do you know of any gallery there that exhibits or has exhibited his work?"

"I've never heard of one."

"Serena mentioned the name Duncan, but I checked, and there's no listing for a gallery with that name or anything similar."

Mira frowned. "Duncan?"

"Does the name mean something to you?"

"I'm not sure. It rings a bell, but . . . no, I'm drawing a blank. My memory isn't what it used to be."

"Will you think about it? Let me know if you remember?"

"Of course."

Jessie paused to frame what she wanted to say next. "Mira, I wouldn't ask you this, but you did say you don't like Dalishar. If you'd rather not answer, I'll understand."

"Go ahead."

"Do you think it's possible he's mixed up in something shady?"

"What do you mean by shady?"

"Anything illegal or quasi-legal."

"That's an interesting question." Mira considered it, stroking the Sheltie's ruff. "Let's say I wouldn't give him a cash donation to deposit with Indian Relief."

"But you haven't heard any rumors or speculations about him?"

"Nothing specific, no. I could ask around, discreetly."

"Would you? As soon as possible?"

"A question for you, first. Do you think Frank Court might be mixed up with Dalishar in something shady?"

Jessie hesitated. "Without going into details, yes."

"And you're afraid of getting hurt."

"Not me, not anymore. Others."

"Other women?"

"Yes."

"I see. Then yes, I will see what I can find out for you."

"*Gracias*, Mira."

"*De nada, mi amiga.* If women like us don't help each other, who will?"

Sarah

Los Alegres, California

SOMEBODY was home now. There was a car parked in the driveway, a light visible through the gathering dusk in one of the side windows. The car was a Toyota compact, probably the schoolteacher's; Scott had a strong preference for BMWs. Was his car in the closed garage? She did not want to go over there if only the new wife was home, and yet neither could she just drive away again, go back to the motel. Her resolve was firmly in place again. And she was cold sober. Do it now, at least get part of it over with.

She left the car, crossed the street, once again climbed the porch steps. Stood stiff and straight as she rang the bell.

Chimes echoed inside, faded to silence. After a few seconds she thought she heard a sharp exclamation, a man's voice; it was followed by more silence. Another sound came then, one she couldn't identify, but there were no approaching footsteps. The door remained closed.

More pressure on the bell.

Silence.

And again.

Silence.

This time she leaned hard on the button, one long steady summons. Still no response.

A telephone began to ring inside.

That brought another exclamation, angry-sounding.

Then a muffled cry.

For God's sake, what was going on in there?

Frustration made her reach down and turn the knob. Locked, of course. She rattled it loudly, jabbed her finger against the bell button once more.

No one came.

The phone stopped ringing.

And then, out of the silence, there was a series of muffled noises, a thud of something heavy hitting wall or floor, a woman's thin cry of pain.

The scream sent chills crawling over Sarah's neck. Her hand was still on the doorknob; she rattled it again, listened, heard nothing, and began to beat on the door with her fist.

Footsteps then, but not coming toward the door—hurrying away to the rear, diminishing. Brief span of silence and then a distant cracking noise, as of wood on wood.

She didn't hesitate; timidity was not one of her shortcomings. She ran down off the porch, around the far corner, and down the driveway to the rear. The back door to the house stood wide open. Thrown open, she thought, by a person in flight—the wood-on-wood crack she'd heard. Purpling twilight filled the yard, made silhouettes of trees and plants; nothing moved anywhere among the shadows. She thought she heard rustling sounds from beyond the fence at the rear, but she couldn't be sure.

Still she didn't hesitate. She crossed quickly to the door and stepped inside.

Morgan

Los Alegres, California

HE was still holding her in an iron grip, spitting nonsense words about half a million dollars into her face, when the doorbell started to ring. The sound startled him, sent a surge of relief through her. He said, "Shit!" and jerked his head back and around, held it cocked like a listening animal.

"Who's that? Who's out there?"

"I don't know—"

"Not him, he wouldn't ring his own doorbell."

The chimes echoed again. Again.

Sudden and shrill, close by, the phone rang.

He said, "Shit!" again, with such explosive vehemence that spittle sprayed her face. His fingers bit into her arms.

The door chimes pealed.

The phone kept ringing.

Somebody began pounding on the front door, loud, insistent.

He added a frustrated growling noise to the cacophony, let go of her, and stepped back. But it was a convulsive movement, as much a shove as a release; her feet slid on the carpet, and she flipped backward, hitting the cushions on her neck and shoulders, bouncing, twisting, then skidding off. She was facedown at an awkward angle when she struck the floor. Pain erupted across the middle of her face, sharp enough to tear loose a half-scream of pain.

She rolled over, dazed, and raised her head. He was still standing there, poised, and now she thought she saw a different look on his dark face, one almost of anguish. He hesitated a moment longer—and then he wasn't there anymore. Running steps punctuated the thudding on the door. More sounds eddied around her, all blending together. Then all she could hear was the blood-pulse in her ears.

Wetness crawled down over her mouth and chin. She lifted onto her knees, swept a hand over her face. Sticky . . . blood. There was a stinging throb of pain when she touched her nose, but the blood dribbled from only one nostril. She put her palms flat on the floor, pushed up. Strength seemed to have deserted her. She quit trying to get up and let herself sag back against the couch; bent forward and lowered her face into her hands without touching her nose.

She wasn't alone anymore. She sensed it even before she heard the steps coming into the room, the shocked exclamation.

"Good Lord!"

Not the bearded man—a woman.

Morgan lifted her head, blinking, trying to focus. Slender blond woman in her thirties. Another stranger. Moving toward her now, dropping to one knee.

"Are you badly hurt?"

"No. Just . . . no."

"All that blood . . ."

"My nose."

"Broken?"

"I don't think so."

"Do you want me to call police emergency?"

"No. Please don't. I'm all right . . . I'll be all right."

"Lean back, tip your head back."

Morgan did that. When she looked again, the woman had disappeared. Water ran and ice rattled in the kitchen. Then the woman was back, a damp cloth in one hand, an improvised icepack in the other.

"Take this, hold it against your nose. It'll stop the bleeding."

She took it, held it gingerly. The woman knelt again and began to swab the blood off her mouth and chin. Morgan sat there like a child and let her do it. The fear was mostly gone now; her thoughts no longer swirled. She had never experienced any kind of physical abuse before, intentional or otherwise, and the effect it had was a kind of numbness underlain with anger and humiliation.

The woman was angry, too. Her voice held a cold fury when she asked, "Who did this to you? Your husband?"

"No."

"If it was . . ."

"Not my . . . not him."

"Who then?"

"Intruder. Stranger."

"Where's your husband? Should I call him?"

"I don't know where he is." The cold had eased the pain in her nose, but her nostrils were still clogged. She breathed deeply through her mouth. "I've never seen you before."

"No, we've never met. My name is Sarah Collins, I'm from Canada—"

"Canada?" The numbness receeded all at once. "Sarah, from Canada?"

"That's right."

"Vancouver?"

"Yes, but how did you—"

Morgan gawped at her. "My God," she said, "my God, you're another one."

"What do you mean, another one?"

"His wives, his victims. Another one of *us*."

Jessie

Santa Fe, New Mexico

L
A Fonda had been full, so she'd reserved a room at one of the smaller hotels near the Loretto Chapel. The first thing she did after she checked in was to help herself to a split of California chardonnay from the mini-bar. Glass in hand, she ordered a club sandwich from room service and then called United to check on times and seat availability of flights from Albuquerque to San Francisco tomorrow. Her third call was to John Dollarhide's home number in Philadelphia.

It was nearly eleven there, and he was home and in bed and grumpy at being disturbed. The grumpiness didn't mean anything; it was part of his nature, and she suspected a cultivated part of his no-nonsense lawyer's persona as well. He was nearing seventy now and showing no signs of slowing down. People who asked him when he was planning to retire were one of his pet peeves. His standard response, delivered in an oratorical courtroom growl, was, "The day after I die."

"I warn you," he said, "if this is a social call I'll hang up on you."

"It's not a social call, John. I need legal advice."

"Yes? You're not in trouble, are you?"

"No, it's nothing like that."

"Then why call me at home, instead of at the office during business hours?"

He liked her, she knew, and despite his growls he wasn't displeased to hear from her. She said in the same no-nonsense tones, "I tried earlier today. You weren't available. You seldom are during business hours, or hadn't you noticed?"

"Bah," he said. "Well, then? What's your problem?"

She told him. As concisely as possible, omitting the details of her affair with Frank Court, but even so it took almost fifteen minutes. He didn't interrupt. When she finished, he cleared his throat and said, "You know I don't handle criminal cases."

"Of course. But you know the law, probably as well as any criminal attorney does."

"I won't deny that. You haven't contacted the authorities yet, I take it."

"No. I wanted to talk to you first."

"Don't," he said. "Not yet. Possibly not for some time."

"I thought that's what you'd say."

"The problem," Dollarhide said, "is that the man appears to be guilty of a number of scattered crimes. The easiest to prove is bigamy, of course, but it's also the least serious and invites potential jurisdictional squabbles. According to what you've told me, charges could be brought against him in four different states and the Dominion of Canada. Even if he were tried and convicted in all five, and that is unlikely, his time in prison would be minimal."

"And the more serious crimes?"

"Well, if—and it's a large *if*—intent to commit fraud can be proven, the case involves the crossing of state lines and an international border, and that makes it a federal matter."

"The FBI."

"Yes. I'm no fan of theirs, Jessie. I disliked Hoover, but he ran the Bureau with a certain degree of efficiency. Efficient isn't a word I'd use to describe it nowadays, particularly since nine-eleven and the focus on antiterrorism. It would take quite a lot to stir their stumps on a nonpolitical, nonviolent, low-profile fraud case. More than what you have so far. The evidence from the safe deposit box is incriminating but not conclusive. At least part of the cash was embezzled from his present wife, certainly, but there is nothing illegal in a community property state like California about a husband controlling jointly held funds, even without the wife's knowledge, unless it's a clear-cut case of intent to defraud. The operative phrase being clear-cut. Without sufficient proof, Morgan Cord is at risk from our good and true friends in the Internal Revenue Service."

"The IRS? Why?"

"It's conceivable they could step in and claim she conspired with her husband to avoid taxes by stockpiling cash, and prosecute her along with him."

"Lovely. The victim victimized again."

"It happens all the time, my dear. You know that as well as I do."

"What about the passports? At least some of them have to be forgeries."

"No doubt. But in this brave new world of ours, the only possessor of forged passports who inspires sharp scrutiny is a known or suspected terrorist. Otherwise, the offense is likely to be regarded as minor."

"The list of names and dollar amounts?"

"Without substantiation," Dollarhide said, "they're open to innocent as well as criminal interpretation."

"So what exactly do we need to stir those official stumps?"

"The man's true identity. Information on his background and any criminal record he might have. The identities of his other victims. Their cooperation in supplying financial records and any other evidence to support the claim of fraud, and most importantly, their willingness to testify against him in court. The more united the front, the stronger the case."

"Which means hiring a good private detective agency. Can you recommend one, John?"

"I can, but I warn you, their fees for this sort of investigation will be expensive."

"I don't care about that. I'll foot the entire bill myself if I have to."

"Indeed?"

"Whoever Frank Court is," Jessie said, "he's gotten away with his vicious racket for at least twenty years. That's twenty years too damn long."

"'The wicked shall flourish like the green bay tree, but they shall be cut down in their prime.'"

"Biblical quote, John? But I admit it's apt."

"My quotes are always apt, especially in a courtroom. Very well, then. The agency is Blakiston Associates, here in Philadelphia. I'll call Harvey Blakiston first thing in the morning and arrange a meeting for early afternoon, if that suits you."

"I'm afraid it doesn't," Jessie said. "I'm not calling from home. I'm in New Mexico at the moment—Santa Fe. Tomorrow I'm thinking of flying out to San Francisco."

"For God's sake, why?"

She told him why.

There was a silence before he said in his stiff-and-stern courtroom voice, "You know, of course, that you're being foolish. This man may well be dangerous. My advice to you is to come straight back here and let Harvey Blakiston handle the investigation."

"Good advice, no doubt," she said, "but I don't think I'm going to take it."

"And why not?"

"I was a passive woman after Darrin's death, a woman I didn't like very much, and Frank Court put an end to that, hands-on. Now I intend to put an end to him the same way."

"I see."

"But you don't approve."

"There are a great many things I don't approve of," Dollarhide said. "If there is one thing I've learned in sixty-eight years of living, it's not to concern myself with those over which I have no control. I've never yet tried to change a woman's mind once it's made up, and I have no intention of starting with you."

"I appreciate that. Does Harvey Blakiston need to talk to me in person before he begins his investigation?"

"Not if you authorize me to act in your behalf."

"You're so authorized."

"Very well. I'll pass along the information you've given me, but he'll certainly have questions. And one thing he'll need immediately is a photograph of the man. The most recent of the passport photos should suffice. Call Morgan Cord and have her send the passport to me by Federal Express first thing tomorrow. Copies of all the other items she found in the safe deposit box as well, including the remaining passports."

"What about the originals?"

"They can remain in her safe deposit box for the time being. As long as she makes sure to keep the key in an equally safe place."

"I'll call her right away," Jessie said. "And call you tomorrow after I arrive in San Francisco to confirm and then get in touch with Harvey Blakiston. My flight gets in at ten-fifteen California time. Will you be in your office between one-fifteen and one-thirty?"

"I can, and I will."

"Thanks, John. For everything."

"You can thank me," Dollarhide said, "by not doing anything to make either of us regret the loss of your passivity."

It was a good exit line, and he knew it; he disconnected without saying good-bye.

A room service waiter arrived with her sandwich just then. She looked at it after he was gone, decided it could wait. One more call first. She poured herself another glass of wine, opened her address book to the new entry for Morgan Cord in Los Alegres, California, and picked up the phone again.

Sarah

Los Alegres, California

THEY sat across from each other at the dinette table in the kitchen. All the talking was finished now, both their stories related in depth; for the moment there didn't seem to be anything more to say. Wind thrummed faintly outside, but the house held a preternatural stillness. There were threads of unease in the quiet, and yet at the same time it was not as strained as it might have been between two strangers; the shattering commonality they shared had created a kind of bleak intimacy.

For a time they just sat there, Sarah staring into her empty glass, Morgan sipping hot coffee and looking sideways at or through her reflection in the dark-backed rear window. Not so much avoiding eye contact as avoiding the obscene little pile in the middle of the table—the photocopies of marriage licenses, passports, snapshots, and the list of names and dollar amounts. Her name, her image among all the others . . . proof to corroborate Morgan's words. Not that the proof had been necessary. All she'd needed had been contained in the words themselves, the dull pain in the woman's voice and expression.

Sarah moved the glass back and forth with her fingertips, smearing wet across the table's surface. The double shot of Scotch had had no effect on her; it might have been plain water. She wanted another, several more . . . and yet she didn't want them. There was not enough liquor to blot out what she had just learned.

How did she feel? She wasn't sure, couldn't analyze her emotions. The shock was gone, and so was the sick, black despair that had briefly followed; now there was acceptance, but no other clear feelings except an angry burning deep inside, like a spot of laser heat. Too soon for anything else, more time needed for processing and developing. Here, at this moment . . . switches flipped off or set at idle. Suspended animation.

After a time she raised her eyes, looked again at Morgan Cord. The icepack had stopped the nosebleed; her nose was still red but not bent or swollen, as it would've been if it were broken. She'd washed her face, exchanged her bloody blouse for a clean white one, run a comb through her hair. Except for the haunted look in her eyes, this would be the way Morgan normally looked—and the effect was disconcerting, because it was like facing an off-image of herself. Same body type, similar facial bone structure, same pale-ash shade of hair, though Morgan's was longer and styled differently. No real resemblance, and yet they might have been related. Sisters. Or—chilling thought—counterparts, reflections of a prototype. Doppelgängers.

Morgan seemed to feel the scrutiny; she turned her head. Their gazes locked, held—scrutiny in return. "Blonds," she said at length. "Pale-eyed blonds."

"I was thinking the same thing."

"Slender, long legs, small breasts."

"Yes. He told me once I matched his vision of the—" The rest of it lodged in Sarah's throat.

"Ideal woman? He said the same to me."

"Most men want variety in their . . . bed partners. Not him, though. He seems to want—"

Again she broke off. Morgan looked away; Sarah did the same. Silence rebuilt. Both of them thinking along similar lines again, probably, and neither wanted the conversation to go there. Had he tried to create bed clones, too? Women who would play the same little intimate games, reprise all the little things he liked? And had he compared them, assigned points for or against, ranked them in order of preference? It was a speculation neither she nor Morgan was ever likely to voice.

Morgan stood, went to the sideboard to refill her cup. She moved stiffly, still hurting from the stranger's abuse, even though she'd made no complaint. Composed now, but with emotions roiling just below the surface—bitterness, anger, hatred, God knew what else. All the feelings Sarah herself would have soon enough. Two of a kind psychologically as well as physically. Emotional, vulnerable, trusting, yet still resilient and strong-willed. Intelligent, if not particularly intuitive. All qualities he seemed to like in his clones, maybe because they provided him with a challenge, a greater thrill. Independent women carefully manipulated until they had been made dependent, drained of pride as well as financial security, and then cast aside in favor of the next victim.

God, she thought, underneath all that superficial charm he must really hate us, all of us, all women.

"Refill, Sarah?"

Yes, she thought. "No," she said.

Morgan sat down again, made eye contact, looked away. New silence. She broke it finally by saying to her reflection in the window glass, "This is so damn awkward."

"We'll get past that," Sarah said.

"I hope so. I'm glad you came."

"So am I. I couldn't have timed it any better."

"Not just for that reason."

"I know. Misery loves company."

"I'm having enough trouble coping," Morgan said. "I can't imagine what it must be like for you . . . believing he was dead, grieving for him, and then being hit with all this. . . ."

"As bad as the truth is, it's better than not knowing."

Faint, bitter smile. "The truth will set you free?"

"I'd like to believe that. It's something to hang onto."

"And we're not alone anymore, that's something else."

"You and me and Jessie Keene. So far."

"It helped, talking to Jessie. But she's thousands of miles away, just a voice on the phone right now. It's not the same as having someone right here."

"One of his other wives, you mean."

"Well, it's not as difficult for her. She didn't have a life with him, doesn't have the time or the . . . emotion invested that we do."

"She wasn't going to marry him, you said?"

"That's what she told me. Too many doubts."

"Then she's a lot smarter than either of us."

Another patch of silence.

Morgan said then, "Four years. Why do you suppose he works on that cycle?"

"The length of time it takes him to drain finances, I suppose. And to get bored with one woman, one place."

"It wouldn't have taken him four years to steal my inheritance," Morgan said bitterly. "He could have had it all in one or less. There must be more to it than that, more than just the money."

"God knows. Sick satisfaction, warped thrill. It's all just a game to a man like him."

"He must really hate women."

"That occurred to me, too. I'm sure he does. But if you asked him, he'd tell you otherwise. He'd say he's given each of us four years of his life, four years of being an attentive, loving husband in exchange for what he took. Value given for value received."

"The fucking you get for the fucking you got."

"Exactly."

"I hate him," Morgan said with sudden vehemence. "For a while after I discovered what he was, there was still some residual love left. Not anymore. I've crossed the line."

Sarah said, "So have I," and it wasn't until she spoke the words that she realized it was true. Eight long years of nurturing and then hopeless love, and in the space of two days it had been kicked and battered into the exact opposite. Such a thin, thin line. It wasn't even a virulent hatred, at least not yet. A cold, almost objective feeling for the man she'd grieved and pined for that just last week would have been unimaginable.

"We can't let him hurt any other women. We have to make him pay for what he's done."

"We will. We'll make him pay, all right."

"If only we had some idea where he is."

"Well, at least we know why he disappeared so suddenly." This time, she added bitterly to herself. "If what the intruder said to you is true about the five hundred thousand dollars."

"The look in his eyes when he said it . . . it's true." Morgan swallowed the last of her coffee. The cup rattled against the saucer when she set it down. "Still, that much money . . . it seems like a fantasy figure. What could Burt possibly be involved in that would bring him half a million dollars?"

"Whatever it is, it's criminal."

"Yes. Not much doubt of that, is there."

No, not much doubt. Four years married, four years pining away . . . for a crook, a criminal, a bigamist, and a con man and God knew what else. It should've been mind-boggling, there should be some sense of denial in her even now. And yet there wasn't. She didn't question his guilt, his wickedness—or the extent of her own gullibility. The evidence was incontrovertible, but it was more than just the evidence. It was as if some seed of knowledge had been planted in her long ago, as if at some visceral level she had known what he was and simply refused to allow the seed to germinate.

". . . seemed to think he might come back here," Morgan was saying.

"I'm sorry, what?"

"The bearded man. He seemed to think there's a chance Burt might come back."

"Not if he knows he's being stalked, he won't."

"He may not know it. Or that I was able to get into his safe deposit box and empty it. I think he'd have contacted me by now if he did."

"You're right. He's not the kind to throw away more than sixty thousand dollars, even if he has half a million. And he'll surely want those passports."

"He won't get any of it, not from me."

"He might try to use force."

"He's never once raised a hand to me. To you?"

"No, but that doesn't mean he wouldn't if he were desperate enough. Or that he hasn't already done physical harm to some other woman. What do we really know about him?"

"Nothing," Morgan admitted. "No more than we know about the bearded man."

Sarah was silent for a time. Then, "I wonder."

"What?"

"If he could be the same man I paid off in Vancouver, the man who told me Scott or whatever his damn name was still alive and where to find him."

"My God, Sarah, is that possible?"

"I don't know. It doesn't make sense that he'd bother to demand five thousand dollars for that kind of information, when the two of them were mixed up together in a half-million-dollar deal. But a lot of things don't seem to make sense anymore. If they're not the same man, then who was the one in Vancouver?"

"And how did he know so much about Burt and me?"

"Well, whoever the intruder is, he's likely to come back here. And he's already shown that he's capable of violence."

"Meaning you think I should move somewhere else for a while? No. I won't be driven out of my home."

"That wasn't what I was going to suggest."

"What, then?"

"Two things. One, a gun for protection."

"I have one." Morgan's mouth bent at the corners. "Burt bought it for me."

"And taught you how to use it, I'll bet."

"At a firing range. I don't like it, I'm not comfortable with guns—"

"I am," Sarah said. "He bought one for me, too, when we were first married."

"Dear Burt," Morgan said acidly. "But I don't think I could shoot someone, even in self-defense."

Sarah said, "You wouldn't have to worry about that if I were here with you."

"Are you offering to stay with me?"

"Well, I think someone should. If not me, a friend."

"There's no one I'd be comfortable with, who'd understand."

"We hardly know each other," Sarah said, "but . . . I don't want to be alone right now, and I don't think you do, either."

"No. I don't."

"Just for tonight, then. Or longer, if we find we can stand each other."

"Moral support. I'd be grateful."

"I took a room at the Sheraton across the river, but it won't take long to drive over and check out and collect my things—"

The telephone interrupted her.

They both jumped at the sudden noise. Morgan said, "I'd better answer, it might be Jessie," and got slowly to her feet.

Amazing, Sarah thought as she watched Morgan pick up the kitchen extension, how calm she was sitting here in the kitchen of another of her bigamous husband's wives, calmly preparing to meet and deal with the biggest of all the crises in her life. For four years she'd existed in fear of everything, including the rest of her life, and now all of a sudden the fear factor seemed to have been bled out of her. Sudden emergency had that kind of profound effect sometimes, like shock therapy.

Sudden truth did, too. Maybe Morgan was right; maybe the truth would set her free.

Jessie

Santa Fe, New Mexico

M Y God, Morgan, he attacked you?"

"Not exactly. Grabbed me, pushed me down over the couch."

"That sounds like an attack to me. Are you all right?"

"Still a little shaken. If it hadn't been for Sarah . . ."

"Right place at the right time," Sarah Collins said. She was on an extension, making it a conference call. Jessie liked her manner and the sound of her voice: calm, steady, no wasted words or unnecessary questions. Either she was congealed enough to have gotten over her shock quickly and cleanly, or her emotions were stored in a thick-walled box inside her. "A few minutes later, and there's no telling what he might've done."

"Did you call the police?" Jessie asked.

"No," Morgan said. "There didn't seem to be much point in it without opening up the whole can of worms. And I couldn't face that tonight."

"It's probably for the best. I spoke to my attorney a few minutes ago, and he agrees that contacting the authorities would be premature, that we need more evidence. . . . I'll get to all that in a minute. What concerns me now is you and Sarah. Suppose the intruder comes back?"

"We don't think he will. But if he does, he'll regret it."

"You're going to stay in the house then?"

"We both are. I won't be driven away from here. This is my home, it's all I have left."

Jessie understood that well enough. Her home in Elton, the house and antique shop, were all she'd had for seven months after Darrin's death. You had to have something tangible, personal, meaningful, to hang on to in a time of crisis; let go of it, for any reason, and the fragile underpinnings of normalcy would crumble and you'd crumble along with it.

She took a long swallow of wine, still trying to put these latest developments—a double jolt, good news and bad news both—into perspective. Sarah Collins's sudden arrival in Los Alegres was like the answer to a prayer: another wife, another victim who expressed the same anger, betrayal, desire for revenge, and who was willing to do something about it. Now they were a unified front of three; strength in numbers, power in numbers. But then Morgan had dropped her bad-news bombshell. Home invasion . . . violence . . . the astonishing figure of five hundred thousand dollars . . . All of that added elements of confusion and menace to what had seemed to be a fairly clear-cut string of nonviolent, white-collar crimes; hinted at darker, even uglier offenses beneath the surface.

"Morgan, you're sure you've never seen the intruder before?"

"Positive. I'd remember if I had."

Sarah said, "It's possible he's the same man who sold me the information in Vancouver that brought me down here. But it just doesn't seem likely."

"No, it doesn't. At least, not based on what we know now."

"Which leaves us with two mysterious strangers instead of one."

"Two strangers and one alias, all of them crooks."

"Alias?"

"I can't think of him as Frank Court any longer," Jessie said. "He's just one long string of aliases."

"I can't think of him as Scott Collins, either."

"'Alias' fits him," Morgan said. "The alias man."

Jessie said, "I can't get over that half-a-million-dollar figure. Did the intruder say anything about where the money might've come from?"

"Not a word."

"Well, it's not any legal windfall, that's for sure. Some kind of scam. But what kind produces such a huge payoff? And why would he need a partner?"

"It doesn't even seem to be in character for him," Sarah said. "From what we know, he's spent most of his life slowly bilking five- and six-figure amounts out of women like us . . . a small-time, not a high-powered con man."

"Something he stumbled into?" Morgan said.

"Or has been planning for a long time."

"Blackmail? Extortion?"

"I wouldn't put anything past him," Jessie said. "And what does seem to be in character is double-crossing this partner of his and keeping all the money for himself."

"That might explain why he disappeared so suddenly, why he hasn't come back for the money in his safe deposit box."

"And why he didn't bother to follow up with me after the big rush," Jessie agreed. "The payoff must've come after he left New Mexico. With five hundred thousand dollars, he doesn't need to bother with another wife."

Sarah said, "Unless she was very rich. Then he'd bother."

"Met someone like that, you mean? Swept her off her feet?"

"His modus operandi, isn't it?"

"But no woman in her right mind would hand over half a million dollars in cash to a man she's just met, not for any reason."

"You're right, it doesn't seem likely. And where would the bearded man fit into something like that?"

". . . Did you say bearded?"

"The intruder," Morgan said. "Didn't I mention that he had a beard?"

"No, you didn't." But the thought, the possibility, had been in her mind just the same, from the moment the bombshell had been dropped. Now it was full-born. "A full beard, thick, wiry?"

". . . Yes."

"Piercing eyes, light blue, almost gray? Longish black hair? About forty?"

"My God, you know who he is?"

"Dalishar," she said.

Morgan

Los Alegres, California

It was Sarah who found the second key.

They went into Burt's—into Alias's—study to see if something might give them a clue to what he was up to. Dalishar had hurled papers and things around, but the only real damage was to the painting of the ghouls feeding in the graveyard; it had been ripped off the wall and the frame smashed, the canvas torn into ribbons. The reason for that was plain enough when Morgan found a fragment that bore the artist's name. Dalishar. His rage and frustration had carried over to his own work. She'd thought that the name sounded vaguely familiar. *The Devouring*. Dear God.

The room gave Sarah an eerie feeling, she said as they searched it. It was more or less a carbon copy of his study in their Vancouver home, down to the same style and color of desk and the type of artwork. He'd had macabre paintings there, too. For all his serial changing of wives and environments, he was the kind of regimented man who required familiar surroundings and the same lifestyle no matter where he was or who he was living with.

There was nothing else there to connect Alias and Dalishar, unless it was stored on the computer. And unless the second key, found among the odds and ends in the hand-carved teak box where Morgan had found the safe deposit key, had some significance. This one was much smaller, of a different shape, and attached to a quarter-sized wire ring. Morgan had simply overlooked it on Saturday; the envelope with the bank key had claimed all her attention.

When Sarah plucked it out of the box, she asked, "What's this for?"

"I don't know. I don't think I've ever seen it before."

"Looks like a padlock key. Does he keep anything padlocked in the house or garage?"

"Just the back gate. It opens onto a creek bed, and there's a park beyond that."

"Let's see if the key fits that lock."

It didn't.

"The farm," Morgan said when they were back inside the house. "There's a padlock on the door of that cinder-block building I told you about."

"Do you remember what kind? This key is for a Yale."

"No. I didn't look closely."

Sarah said, "If he went there often, he'd likely keep a key with him. But this could be an extra—shiny, no scratches. Most padlocks come with two."

"We could drive out there in the morning and check."

"I think we should. I'd like to know what's inside that building."

"I would, too. But what if someone's there?"

"Alias? I'd like it if he were."

"Or Dalishar. Or the owner of the woman's clothing, whoever she is." Not Dalishar's girlfriend; Jessie had told them the clothing in the duffel bag was nothing like the kind Serena wore.

"We'll take the gun along for protection," Sarah said. "I don't know about you, but I can't just sit around waiting for something else to happen."

Morgan nodded. She'd been overemotional all her life, and whether she wanted to admit it or not, one of those strong emotions had been fear. Not of physical harm—she wasn't a coward; of change, of risk, of strong commitment to anyone other than Burt . . . Alias . . . or anything other than her profession. Of being hurt the way he had hurt her. All her life she had rebelled against that damned Germaine Greer argument, and at this major crisis point, in spite of all her earlier protestations to the contrary, she was in danger of emotionally crippling herself. Either she channeled all her feelings, all her passions, into this fight—no waffling, no looking back, and to hell with the consequences—or she would live the rest of her life as another Tepid Tolliver.

"Neither can I," she said. "Much better if we make it happen ourselves."

✦

Noises in the night. Thumps, creaks, rustles, wind sounds. They woke her from restless periods of half-sleep, kept her awake at intervals. But not because they stoked her imagination; she knew them for what they were. She was at that fatigue point where neither mind nor body could rest completely, where every sense seemed heightened and her skin had a tingling, prickly feel. Even the pain in her nose, dull and barely noticeable before she went to bed, seemed magnified in the darkness.

Thoughts and questions swam through her consciousness in a jumbled loop; she couldn't seem to grasp any of them for long. They swam through her unconscious as well, humid and surreal dream images that were gone as soon as she woke up. The man named Dalishar loomed no larger than any of the others. He wasn't half the threat to her that Alias was in so many ways; all he was after was money. He hadn't even broken into the house, had simply walked in through the unlocked back door; she and Sarah had made sure all the doors and windows were secure before they came upstairs. And Sarah was in the next room, the ugly little .32 caliber revolver on the nightstand beside the bed.

Sarah. And Jessie Keene. One woman she'd known less than twelve hours, the other she'd yet to set eyes on, and she felt closer to them, was able to confide in them more easily and trusted them more, than Laurel or Becky or her parents. Odd the way circumstances could create strong bonds among strangers, change outlooks, lifelong patterns and habits almost overnight. She was not the same woman she'd been last week, or even yesterday. Neither was Sarah. Neither was Jessie.

That was one good thing Alias had done for them, maybe the only important thing. He'd opened each of them up, made each come to terms with who they were and what they were made of.

Wednesday, May 21

Sarah

Sonoma County, California

THEY left the house together shortly before nine o'clock. Cold, foggy morning—just like home. But the weather no longer depressed her, nor would it when she returned to Vancouver. And right now any kind of daylight was better than the dark.

She hadn't slept much during the night. Neither had Morgan, judging from the dark smudges under her eyes, a looseness to the skin of her throat and around her mouth—the same outward manifestations of fatigue and stress that had confronted Sarah in the guest bathroom mirror. She felt all right, though. Capable. Ready to face whatever lay ahead.

There had been a little residual awkwardness between Morgan and her at first, but it hadn't lasted long. Their mutual resolve put an end to it. By the time they'd finished coffee and juice and English muffins, they were comfortable enough with each other that the occasional silences were not strained. They said nothing about the bearded man, and little about Alias. The farm, yes—Morgan provided enough detail about the property so Sarah would know what to expect.

They took Sarah's rental car. She was not a good passenger at the best of times; she liked to drive, and she preferred to be the one in control. Morgan had no objection.

First stop was a copy shop downtown, where Morgan made additional copies of the documents from the safe deposit box. Then they drove to the Bank of America branch where Morgan had deposited the originals, to pick up one of the passports—the one with the best photograph of Alias. And from there, to a FedEx outlet where they sent the copies and passport overnight to Jessie's attorney, John Dollarhide, in Philadelphia. He would arrange for copies of the passport photo to be made and passed on to the detective agency Jessie had hired.

No one followed them on their rounds, or out to Highway 101; Sarah made sure of that. Neither of them had much to say after they left Los Alegres. On hold, waiting, occupied with their own thoughts. By the time they reached Coyote Springs Road, the fog had burned off. The early-morning glare led Sarah to shield her eyes behind her dark glasses.

Morgan sat forward, her hands on the dashboard, squinting ahead. "We're almost there. You did bring the gun?"

"In my purse."

"Could you really . . . I mean . . ."

"Shoot somebody? I think so. Yes."

"But could you shoot *him?*"

Could she? She didn't know, didn't want to think about it. She said only, "That's not going to happen."

The fence-post mailbox marked 4320 loomed ahead. Morgan said, "There it is, on the left," and Sarah slowed and made the turn. The deep ruts in the dirt lane forced her to reduce their speed to a crawl. *Be there . . . don't be there.* She was not sure which she wanted more, to get the confrontation with him over and done with or to have it postponed to a different time and place.

Anticlimax. The scene that opened up ahead of them was one of emptiness—house and garage and cinder-block building, an area of dead brown grass, lines of trees. Nothing moved anywhere. And when Sarah stopped the car and they got out, there was nothing to hear except wind-punctuated silence.

"Doesn't look like anyone's here," she said.

"Or been here since I was."

But Morgan was wrong about that. When they went to have a look at the garage, they found that the double doors were no longer locked, and the light-colored car was gone. And when they entered the house, they found no sign of the clothing, leather duffel, or toiletries Morgan had seen the day before. The refrigerator was empty as well, the box of cereal and the bottle of Scotch also gone. Even the soiled glass in the sink had been washed and put away.

"Why would she clean up after herself so thoroughly?" Morgan wondered. "Unless she's one of those compulsive types . . ."

"Maybe she didn't. Maybe somebody wanted to erase all the signs of her visit."

"Somebody?"

"She wasn't the only one here," Sarah said, "before or after you. It's a long way to anything other than another farmhouse. She had to've been driven away and then driven back again—she didn't just walk."

"Alias? Dalishar?"

"Somebody."

"Why would it be necessary for anyone to clean up?"

"Good question. That dark car just leaving when you came yesterday—could the driver have been Alias?"

"I don't think so, but I can't be sure."

"But it was a man?"

"I'm not even sure of that. It could've been a woman."

"The car wasn't familiar?"

"No. Not Alias's BMW, that much I do know."

Outside, they took a quick turn around the squarish cinderblock building. Morgan pointed out the skylights. "I wonder if Alias had them installed."

"It's hard to tell from here, but they don't look particularly new."

"The curtains on the windows do."

"Why put them on? And why lock this building up tight and leave the house wide open?"

At the locked door, Morgan produced the tiny key on its metal ring. Her hand was steady, Sarah noticed, as she probed it into the slot in the padlock. It slid in smoothly, turned smoothly; there was a sharp click, and when she tugged, one of the staples pulled free. She slipped the lock out of the hasp.

"So far so good."

Morgan tried the knob. "Locked. I remember trying it before."

"Let me take a look." Sarah bent to examine the lock, then grasped the knob and shook it. The door wobbled a little, not quite tight in its frame. "We ought to be able to get it open. Wait here."

She went across to the rental car, rummaged around in the trunk. When she came back, she held a tire iron in one hand. She leaned a shoulder against the door, wedged the bladed end of the iron into the crack between the jamb and the door edge above the lock, worked with it until it was set tight, then took a two-handed grip and heaved backward. Wood groaned and metal squeaked, but the lock held.

Again. And again the lock held.

Morgan said, "It'll take both of us," and moved in close to add her double grip to the tire iron. Together they strained with it until the bladed end began to slip free; they wedged it back in and tried again. This time there was a low ripping sound. One more sharp tug, and the locking bolt tore loose from the plate, splintering the jamb. The door scraped inward a few inches.

Sarah stepped inside first, still clutching the tire iron. Massed shadow and shapes half-seen in the dusty light filtering through the skylights. Morgan, following, said, "There must be a light switch. . . . Here."

Fluorescent light from half a dozen hanging fixtures overhead threw the interior into sudden bright relief.

Morgan caught her breath. Sarah said, "My God."

One big, bare-walled, concrete-floored room with a clay-spattered bench on the left—probably a former owner's workshop and potting room. Now it was something else entirely. The only furniture it contained was three tables of varying sizes, all of them old and scarred, the kind of pieces that you could buy in junk shops or at garage sales; their tops were covered with palettes, mortars and pestles, and other mixing equipment, and scores of tubes, jars, tins, and bottles of various sizes. The rest of the space, except for one section in front of the middle window, contained rolled, paint-stained dropcloths; three easels—one empty, one collapsed, one bearing a cloth-draped work in progress; a stack of blank canvases, a grouping of faded, cracked paintings in cheaply ornate frames, another grouping of unframed prints and lithographs, and a row of complete and partially complete paintings on stretched canvas.

An art studio. A well-stocked, commercial-type art studio on a rented farm in an isolated rural section of the county.

Jessie

San Francisco, California

San Francisco had changed in the ten years since she'd last been there. From an airplane window, and at a distance through the windshield of her rental car, it owned the same scenic charm; but once she was into it, the city had a shabby, depressing aspect. Littered streets, great numbers of homeless, a man openly urinating on the sidewalk near the cable car turnaround at Powell and Market.

Had the city really changed so much, she wondered as she drove across Market and turned west on Ellis Street, or were her perceptions warped by rose-colored memories? The other three, no, four times she'd visited San Francisco, Darrin had been with her. Drinks and dinner at the Top of the Mark, afternoons at the museums, on bay cruises and a tour of Alcatraz, evening prowls through North Beach and Chinatown . . . good times, fine, bright memories. The city had certainly had its flaws on those occasions; she simply hadn't noticed them, or hadn't internalized them if she had. It might well be that coming here alone under the present circumstances had given the surroundings a much bleaker aspect than they deserved. Like looking at a prized antique and ignoring its artistry, seeing only its imperfections.

Another part of the reason could be the weather. It was a cold, blustery day, full of blowing fog. No city, large or small, was at its best cloaked in various tones of gray, not even a fog-famous metropolis like San Francisco.

No matter in any case. Neither the weather nor her negative impressions had dampened her spirits. She was glad to be back here, energized by purpose and eager for the planned meeting later in the day with Morgan and Sarah. Now they were a united front of three—three victims, three avengers. Harvey Blakiston and his investigators had begun the search for Alias's true identity and the identities of his other victims—she'd spoken to him on the phone this morning, on the drive from Santa Fe to Albuquerque—and thanks to Mira Ortiz, she had what seemed to be a solid lead to Dalishar and perhaps Alias. The net had been spread and would keep spreading.

But Dalishar's invasion of Morgan's home and the mysterious five-hundred-thousand-dollar scam, if that was what it was, were disturbing complications. Violence begat violence; it wasn't inconceivable that Morgan, or Sarah, or even herself, could be caught in harm's way. If Alias really had gotten hold of such a huge amount of cash, it was also not inconceivable that he might wriggle free of the net and manage to disappear again without a trace. Money, if you had enough of it, could buy you anything in this world; that had been proven to her over and over in recent years, by high-profile criminal trials and all sorts of corporate and political chicanery. The prospect of that happening, of Alias being free to one day find another woman to charm and victimize, was so intolerable that she felt she would do anything, take any risk, to prevent it from happening. That was the primary reason she was here in California, against the advice of both John Dollarhide and Harvey Blakiston.

After her early-morning talk with Mira Ortiz, she'd rushed to catch a noon flight out of Albuquerque. It was a few minutes before one now. The sooner she paid a call at the Duncombe School of Modern Art, the better.

"It's Duncombe, not Duncan," Mira Ortiz had said to her on the phone. "The Duncombe School of Modern Art on Larkin Street in San Francisco."

"An art school?"

"Run by a woman named Ellen Duncombe. An artist herself, and evidently not a very good one, which of course is why she teaches."

"The woman you overheard Dalishar talking about?"

"Must be. Sam Hazelrigg mentioned her to me once—that was what I couldn't remember last night. It seems Dalishar tried to talk Sam into exhibiting some of her paintings, as a favor. Sam refused. Strictly imitative work, he said."

"When was this?"

"About three years ago."

"What's her relationship with Dalishar?"

"More professional than personal, according to Sam," Mira said. "She's older than Dalishar, mid- to late forties. And nothing at all the slinky, sexy, Serena type he seems to prefer. Sam also got the impression she might be a lesbian."

"Could she be Dalishar's patron, do you think?"

"I guess it's possible. Depends on how successful her art school is."

"Does Sam know anything else about her?"

"No. Met her only that one time."

"Her school is on Larkin Street, you said?"

"Nineteen twenty-eight Larkin. I looked it up on the Net for you."

Ellis Street, at least in the blocks close to Market, was something of a downtown slum. Dirty streets, urban-blighted buildings, men and women drinking in little groups or sprawled in doorways or pushing shopping carts full of recyclables and personal possessions. The area improved as she neared Larkin, a couple of blocks east of Van Ness Avenue, and turned north—an average urban neighborhood, as far as she could tell, edging onto the downscale side. Nineteen twenty-eight was near Geary—one of a number of nondescript two-story commercial buildings. Jessie found a place to park half a block away.

A secondhand bookshop occupied the downstairs space. A sign in one of the windows above read RAYLYNN STUDIO—INTERPRETATIVE DANCE.

Frowning, she checked the number again: 1928. Had Mira gotten the address wrong somehow? She checked the buildings on both sides. None of those housed the Duncombe art school or any other business related to art. She went back and entered the musty-smelling bookshop. Behind a cluttered counter, a balding middle-aged man stood pricing a stack of Western Americana titles.

"Excuse me," she said, "but I'm looking for the Duncombe School of Modern Art. I was told it was at this address."

"Gone," he said.

"Gone? I don't—"

"Six months ago, about. Damn shame, too. Prospective artists are a lot quieter than interpretative dance students."

"You mean Ellen Duncombe moved her school to a different location?"

"Not as far as I know."

"Closed it then? Why?"

He shrugged. "Why does any small business go belly-up? Not enough customers, not enough income to pay the bills. She must've had more than her share of creditors."

"Why do you say that?"

"Here one day, gone the next."

"No notice? She didn't say anything to you about shutting down?"

"Nope. Busted her lease, though. Landlord wasn't too happy about it."

"How long was she in business here?"

"At least six years. She was here when I took over this shop."

"How well did you know her?" Jessie asked.

"Not very. Say hello to. Not a book person, and didn't like men much, if you know what I mean. At least not men who weren't wannabe artists."

"Do you know where she lives?"

"Nope. I didn't ask, she didn't tell."

"Would you have a phone directory I can look at?"

The request produced a sigh, but he lifted one out from under the counter. She flipped through the white pages to the D's. Damn. No Ellen Duncombe, no listing for anybody named Duncombe.

She closed the directory. "What's your landlord's name?"

"Everett Youd, Youd Realty. Why?"

"He'll have her home address."

"Sure," the bald man said, and laughed. "But if you can get an address, or even a kind word, out of that old fart, you're a better man than I am."

"Just may be that I am," Jessie said seriously. "Where can I find Everett Youd?"

Morgan

Sonoma County, California

THE big room wasn't as haphazardly cluttered as it first seemed. The various paintings and prints and lithographs, the frames and empty canvases, were set out in neat rows. The supplies on the tables—mixed paints, powdered pigments, oils and turpentine, brushes of different sizes, esoteric ingredients such as a jar of white milky fluid labeled *feigemilch* that meant nothing to Morgan—had been carefully arranged, the tubes and jars tightly closed and placed in wooden trays, the brushes and mixing equipment all cleaned. The dropcloths were rolled. The only thing out of place, in fact, was the collapsed easel; it lay on the section of bare concrete in front of the middle window.

Morgan said as they went to look at the paintings, "I don't understand this. Why would Alias want an art studio way out here? He doesn't paint. At least he doesn't as far as I know."

"Maybe it's Dalishar's."

"He lives in New Mexico, Jessie said."

"She also said he spends a lot of time out here."

"But an entire studio? All these paintings and materials, three easels . . ."

"Let's have a look at the paintings."

The prints and lithographs were mostly of lesser-known works by a variety of French Impressionists and Postimpressionists such as

Renoir, Cézanne, Manet, and Chagall, and American jazz age, grass-roots, and social realists such as Wyeth, Hopper, Grant Wood, Robert Hart Benton, Franz Kline. There were also a handful of Surrealist and macabre paintings that didn't belong with the rest, among them two that Morgan recognized as the work of Hieronymus Bosch.

Sarah had plucked out one of the latter group and was staring at it with distaste. Morgan, at a closer glance, saw why. "I've seen that before," she said.

"Goya's *Madhouse*."

"All those hideous faces . . . it reminds me of that thing of Dalishar's."

"A favorite of Alias's when we were together. He gave me a lithograph of it one Christmas that I'm going to burn when I get home." Sarah shivered. "I can't stand Goya."

The old, framed paintings were all still lifes, seascapes, portraits, most of them cracked, pitted, age-toned. Morgan's knowledge of art was limited, but she was sure that none was of any quality or value. They struck her as the kind of paintings you found hanging in junk shops and antique collectives, displayed for their age and ornate frames rather than for their minimal artistic content. She said as much to Sarah, who nodded agreement.

"Why would anyone bother to buy up this many old paintings?"

"For the frames, maybe."

"They don't seem to be any more valuable than what's in them."

"No, they don't."

The better-quality paintings were fewer, all either copies of the early-twentieth-century prints and lithographs or in a similar style. All except two, one of which appeared to be a less than successful attempt to imitate Bosch and the other clearly Goyaesque. Not *Madhouse*—but something just as darkly horrific. Judging from *The Devouring* and what Jessie had told them about his other work, both might have been painted by Dalishar. The others, though . . . Several were unfinished, as if abandoned for some reason; one bore a slash of red paint, as though the artist had deliberately defaced it in a fit of pique.

Morgan removed the cloth shrouding one of the easels. What was propped there was a large sketch done in oils on scraped canvas, unfinished, the background merely brushstrokes in pastel washes, in the foreground a reclining nude and a leering old man peering at her from behind a tree.

"I don't recognize this one," she said.

"No."

"Seems like an odd way to paint. Sketched out that way . . . it almost looks traced."

"So it does," Sarah agreed. "How good do you think these finished paintings are?"

"I'm not much of a judge. Competent, at least."

"If they're good, really good . . ."

"I know. I'm thinking the same thing."

"We could take some of them to a gallery or appraiser—but how would we explain where we got them? No matter what we said, it would be liable to raise suspicions."

Morgan said hesitantly, "I know somebody who might be able to tell us."

"You do?"

"He teaches at my school. Art, among other subjects. He knows quite a bit about fine art and art history."

"Do you trust him?"

". . . As much as I trust any man right now."

"How much would we have to tell him?"

"Nothing about Alias. The paintings—he'd examine them as a favor, and I don't think he'd make an issue of it. Alex isn't that type of person. He's sensed there have been problems in my life lately, and he's been supportive without prying—" Morgan broke off. Why was she going on about Alex Hazard? "I think we should take some of the paintings and leave right now," she said. "This place is starting to get to me."

"Me, too." But her attention now was on the section of bare concrete where the collapsed easel lay. "There's something about that easel. . . ."

"What?"

"I don't know."

Sarah went to where it lay. After a moment, Morgan followed. One of the legs was broken, and one corner of the frame was splintered, as if the easel had been violently thrown or knocked to the floor. Next to the other leg was a long brownish splotch. Sarah knelt to peer at it.

"What is that?" Morgan said. "It doesn't look like paint."

"It's not. It's blood, dried blood."

Jessie

San Francisco, California

YOUD Realty was on Geary Boulevard, half a mile or so west of Japantown. Unimposing place—a storefront between an Asian restaurant and a bicycle shop, its plate-glass window filled with the usual listings boards and a sign that read "Specialists in Rental Properties." The interior was long and narrow, divided by a railing into two sections. Only two of the six desks were occupied, one of them, fortunately, by Everett Youd.

He was a sinewy little man in his fifties, with a skimpy upper lip adorned by an equally skimpy mustache and a speedbump head—Jessie's term for a knobby, ridged skull—over which eleven or twelve dyed hairs had been combed in a crosshatch pattern. He was all smiles and unctuous professional charm until he discovered that she wasn't there to rent, buy, or sell real estate. Then he reverted to what was undoubtedly his true self: a cold, narrow-eyed, barely civil moneygrubber who wouldn't give anybody anything unless there was a profit in it.

"I'm afraid I can't help you," he said. "Our policy is not to give out personal information about our clients, past or present."

"I'm not asking for personal information, Mr. Youd. I have all the personal information about my sister that I need. I'm asking only for her home address."

"Ellen Duncombe is your sister?"

"Estranged. Nine years now."

"I'm sorry to hear that," he lied. "But I still can't give out—"

Jessie said glibly, "It doesn't matter who was at fault for the rift. Suffice it to say that the one family trait we were both born with is stubborness. The estrangement, in my uncle's view, has gone on much too long. His death was the impetus for my trip here from Pennsylvania. That, and the contents of his will."

"Ah, yes. But—"

"He left his entire estate to my sister and me," Jessie said, and added, with just the right amount of bitterness, "Equal shares. But there is a contingency."

"There often is."

"So I'm told. In our case, it is that Ellen and I reconcile and remain reconciled for a minimum of one year. To Uncle John's way of thinking, the best way to accomplish that would be for us to occupy his home in Bucks County for that one year. Together. This presents no problem, in his view, inasmuch as I am a widow and Ellen is unmarried."

"Yes, but why tell me all this? I've already made it clear that our agency policy prohibits—"

"What would you have me do, Mr. Youd? I'm sure Ellen lives somewhere in San Francisco, but I have no idea where. She isn't listed in the telephone directory. She no longer operates her art school. I don't know any of her friends or students. And I've never been in this city before—a stranger in a strange land. How am I to find my sister without your help?"

"Well, you could hire someone, a detective—"

Jessie gave him an appalled look. "And pay God knows how much for information you could give me simply by checking your computer records? I'm not a wealthy woman . . . yet. Nor am I a fool."

Youd didn't know what to say to that. He cleared his throat, tugged at an ugly painted tie, looked at the wall next to his desk, and kept silent.

"Mr. Youd," Jessie said, "I won't appeal to your sense of generosity and fair play, since I assume you have neither. Suppose we put my request on a business basis instead."

"Business basis?" Magic words. She thought she saw his ears twitch. "Are you offering to pay *me* for the information?"

"In a sense. I wouldn't insult you by offering a small amount of cash, but I will promise you this: If you give me my sister's address, I'll see to it that you benefit handsomely for the favor."

"Yes? How so?"

"Once I tell Ellen about the terms of Uncle John's will, she'll have to leave San Francisco and return to Pennsylvania with me. For at least a year. You do see what that means, don't you?"

Youd saw, all right. "Ah," he said.

"Exactly. She will have to either sell or lease her home here. You would like to be the listing agent, I'm sure."

"Of course, of course," Youd said. "But, ah, I must confess that Ms. Duncombe and I are not on the best of terms. She defaulted on her lease of the Larkin Street property, you see. As I recall, there was an unfortunate exchange of words at our last meeting."

"Past history, Mr. Youd. Not relevant. I can and will guarantee that Ellen will list her home with your agency, sell or lease."

"After such a long estrangement, how can you guarantee to exert that much influence with your sister?"

"I've always been able to bend her to my will. Her resentment of the fact was one of the reasons for the rift between us."

"I see." Youd oozed professional charm again. "Well, I certainly appreciate your candor, Mrs. Keene. And the business opportunity."

"Her address, please."

"Yes, yes, of course." Youd called up Ellen Duncombe's file on his computer. "Seventy-nine sixty-nine Quintara Street."

Jessie repeated it. "And where would that be, exactly?"

"Out near the Great Highway and Ocean Beach. Just a few miles from here, very easy to find."

He wrote down directions and then handed her not one but two of his business cards—"one for you, one for your sister." He clasped her hand in both of his damp bony ones and thanked her and said he hoped to see her again and looked forward to hearing from Ellen.

The first thing Jessie did when she got outside was to scrub her hand with her handkerchief. The second thing was to tear up Everett Youd's business cards, both of them, and dump the pieces into a trash receptacle.

✦

Ellen Duncombe's house was in the last block of Quintara Street, near where it dead-ended at the Great Highway. It was a neighborhood of older homes of both funky and conservative architectural styles, no two alike. Number 7969 was a weathered, brown-shingled cottage squeezed so tightly between a two-unit apartment building and a bulging pile of a house with both cupolas and portholes that it seemed trapped there.

Jessie parked across the street. She could hear the boom of the surf when she left the car, but the fog was so thick and roiling here that most of the highway was obscured, and all of the beach and ocean beyond were invisible. She pulled her coat collar up and ducked her neck down into it as she hurried across the street. A concrete walk bordered by two slender rows of artichoke plants led in to a narrow front porch, across which was a wrought-iron security gate that might as well not have been there because the gate stood open.

Somebody was home: In one of the facing windows, light showed palely behind monk's-cloth curtains. Jessie stepped through the open gate. There was no doorbell, so she rapped sharply on the wood panel. She had to knock twice more before the door rattled open and a woman stared out at her. Jessie stared, too, and with considerably more surprise.

The woman was neither Ellen Duncombe nor a stranger.

Dalishar's vampirish girlfriend, Serena.

Sarah

Los Alegres, California

THE bloodstain didn't have to mean anything ominous. It could have come from a nosebleed, a cut finger. And there was only that one dried splotch, large though it was. The collapsed easel and the fact that there was no dropcloth underneath it didn't have to mean anything, either. Nothing else in the cinder-block building, nothing in the house or garage, suggested violence. Jumping to conclusions based on circumstantial evidence was a mistake; she and Morgan agreed on that.

But in the car, on the way back to Los Alegres, Sarah could not get the notion out of her mind that someone had been hurt or worse in that makeshift studio. Alias? She hoped not. Love had crossed the thin line to hate, but the hate was cold and bitter, not hot and ruthless. She wanted him caught and punished, she wanted him to suffer some of the same terrible anguish he'd put her through, but she did not want him dead or physically injured. Strange dichotomy, but there it was. She would spit in his face if he stood before her, unharmed; she would cry, she knew she would break down and cry like a fool, if the next time she saw him he was in a hospital bed or a coffin.

She wondered if Morgan felt the same way. If so, she was no more ready to share her feelings than Sarah was.

One thing they both knew for certain: the art studio, the paintings, *did* mean something ominous. She had a pretty good idea what it was, and she thought Morgan did too, but they weren't ready to discuss that yet, either. Not until they had a better idea of the nature of the eight finished paintings, six large and two small, that they'd loaded into the trunk of the car along with the unfinished nude, the defaced canvas, and a couple of the old, framed oils.

As they were leaving the farm, Morgan used her cell phone to call Los Alegres High School and leave a message for Alex Hazard. He returned the call before they reached Santa Rosa. She didn't tell him much, just that she and a friend from Canada had come into possession of some paintings and wanted to know more about them; would he mind looking at them as soon as possible? He didn't question her. He would cancel his one o'clock class, he said, and meet them at his home in half an hour.

He was waiting when they reached the modest split-level house on a hillside above the high school. Sarah liked him from the first; quiet, intelligent, a man who had been hurt as they had been hurt—Morgan had told her about his wife's infidelity—and whose pain still showed in his eyes. A man who took unusual situations in stride without giving vent to his curiosity. She no longer fully trusted first impressions, but she sensed that in Alex Hazard's case, he was pretty much what he seemed to be—a decent man and a dependable friend.

He was also in love with Morgan.

Sarah knew that inside of five minutes. His feelings were plain in the way he looked at her, the subtle change in his voice when he spoke to her. The same kind of wistful, patient, ever-hopeful love, Sarah thought wryly, as David's for her. But she doubted that Alex, unlike David, had ever voiced it; Morgan seemed unaware of how he felt. Either that, or she sensed it but refused to acknowledge it even to herself. A one-man woman, Morgan. Just as Sarah had always believed herself to be.

Alex helped them carry the paintings into the house. A large enclosed side porch, windowed on two sides to let in a maximum amount of light, served as a combination office and studio. Watercolor paints and brushes and a draped easel testified to his own artistic endeavors, though none of his finished work was in evidence. Lack of apparent vanity—another positive trait. He propped the paintings side by side against one wall and a long couch, frowning as he glanced from one to another.

"I want to examine these more closely," he said to Morgan, "before I make any judgments."

"Without us looking over your shoulder?"

"If you wouldn't mind waiting in the living room, or out on the deck . . ."

They sat at a glass-topped table on a narrow rear deck. It had turned into a sunny day here, the sky clear except for a few shredded-tissue clouds, and there was a broad view of the valley in which Los Alegres nestled, the line of already browning tree-spotted hills to the east, the smudged silhouette of a mountain farther north. Nothing like the spectacular vistas she was used to in Vancouver and the rest of B.C., but appealing in a different, quiet way. But the best thing about the area, right now, was that it was warm here. Not warm enough to banish the chill of the long winter, the bone-deep chill of Alias, but the sun's heat helped.

It was forty-five minutes before Alex reappeared. His face was set into neutral planes, but his eyes showed a grim concern. He beckoned them into the house, led the way into his studio. The paintings were set out in a different order than before, propped so that oblique slants of sunshine lighted them.

"Do you want to tell me where you got these?" he asked Morgan.

"I . . . we'd rather not, Alex. Not now."

"But they did all come from the same place? A private studio somewhere?"

"Yes."

"I thought so." He was silent for a few seconds, as if organizing his thoughts. "All of the unframed paintings here appear to be the work of established artists, similar in form and content to recognized pieces. It's possible a couple of them may actually be originals; I'm not an expert, so I can't really be sure. If they're not originals, they're remarkably good imitations. The other finished ones strike me as less accomplished and almost certainly fakes. The defaced Renoir shows obvious flaws in technique, probably why it was red-lined and scrapped by the artist.

"All right. Lots of amateurs and novices copy the works of established artists, for various reasons—analysis of form and technique, interest in the subject matter, simple admiration. Usually they make exact copies of well-known and obscure works, but sometimes the imitations are stylistic—the new artist utilizes some or all of the techniques of the established one, but adapts them to his own vision and theme. In both those cases the artists almost always use new canvases. All of the paintings here were done on old canvases, either ones that were scraped clean first or over existing oils. As far as I can tell none is an exact duplicate of any one work; they're composites, made from elements of various sizes and proportions traced from different paintings by the same artist from the same period, then cobbled together with great attention to detail. You can see how it's done in this unfinished variation on Thomas Benton's *Persephone*—the tracings in the background and foreground around the reclining nude and the old man."

"Forgeries," Morgan said.

"That's my guess. Created with intent to defraud." He paused for a moment to measure their reactions. "Neither of you seems surprised," he said. "It's what you expected to hear?"

"More or less," Sarah said.

"You realize the potential repercussions? We're talking a major felony here."

"Just how major?"

"Are there any more paintings besides these?"

"Yes. Quite a few more."

"Then it's very serious. How much do you know about art forgery? In general, I mean."

Morgan said, "Not very much."

"I'll give you a little background then. It's a multimillion-dollar business worldwide and has been for decades. Every week there's a news story about some forgery being discovered or someone being duped. Some experts think there may be almost as many bogus and doctored pieces as genuine paintings hanging in museums and private collections and circulating in the art world. The former head of the Metropolitan Museum of Art, Thomas Hoving, once said that of the more than fifty thousand works of art in all fields that he's examined, some forty percent were either phonies or so completely restored or misattributed that they might as well have been forgeries.

"Organized rings turn out fakes by the carload. Even individuals working alone can create astonishing numbers of them. A New

York paintings restorer named Frank X. Kelly produced hundreds of forged Impressionist and Postimpressionist works in his life- time—Manet, Renoir, Grant Woods, Thomas Cole, even Claude Monet, who is considered to be the hardest Impressionist to forge because of the subtlety of his colors and light effects. Kelly bought up old canvases of all sizes at antique shops and either scraped them or painted over them in both watercolors and oils, with every kind of subject matter from still lifes to landscapes to nudes. He was so adept that he worked almost as fast as an authentic artist, with the same ease and tempo, turning out up to ten finished paintings a month and selling them to collectors and unscrupulous dealers for a thousand to fifteen hundred dollars each. He made a small fortune in the racket. And his fakes were so good, there's speculation that some of them have yet to be unmasked, and may never be. . . .

"Well, you get the idea. I've done a lot of reading on the sub- ject, and I tend to get carried away when I talk about it. The point is, there are hundreds of well-known artists, and countless thou- sands of collectors and dealers, hungry for original art. Big profits at little expense, that's the lure."

"How much are fakes like these worth?" Morgan asked.

"I can't answer that. The worth of any successful forgery de- pends on a lot of different factors—the original artist, the scarcity of his work, how wealthy the buyer and how much he or she wants a particular work."

"You said a couple of these might be originals?"

"Might be but probably aren't, given the rest. Good enough to pass in some circumstances, though, if I'm any judge." Alex indi- cated one of the canvases propped on the couch. "This Chagall, for one. If it's a phony, considerable work went into it. Elements from at least three of his Cubo-Futurist religious works, mainly *The Ap- parition,* look to be skillfully blended—two angelic muses here in- stead of one. An earlier or later interpretation of *The Apparition,* which might conceivably have been done at the same approximate time.

"This Manet here might also pass for an original. The Edward Hopper, too, possibly." He indicated a corner on the Hopper paint- ing. "See there, where I scraped away a small portion of the new paint? The old, faded paint is visible underneath."

Sarah said, "That explains the cheap framed paintings."

"Yes. Worthless junkshop art, but done in the same time period."

"Were all these painted by the same artist?" Morgan asked.

"Difficult to say. But my guess is that there's at least two. This painting over here has a much darker theme than any of the others—classic Spanish, not American or French Impressionist or Realist. A Goya knockoff. One of his 'black paintings,' *Witches' Sabbath,* was the primary model."

"Would the Chagall or Hopper or Manet fool a dealer or collector?"

"Well, P. T. Barnum was right, wasn't he," Alex said wryly. "A lot of people are born to be fooled, even knowledgeable people. Need, speed, and greed are the three bywords in a successful art scam. If the mark is gullible enough, hungry enough, maybe larcenous enough, and the seller's package is airtight, any high-quality forgery will pass for an original."

"Seller's package?"

"A plausible explanation of where the pieces came from, how they fit into the canon of surviving works by the same artist, false letters of provenance, that kind of thing. The forger has to give his work an air of conviction, a sense of authenticity, to keep the buyer from noticing any flaws or defects, and that takes a pretty glib presentation."

"And an experienced con man to deliver it," Sarah said. She couldn't quite keep the acid out of her voice.

"Who wouldn't necessarily have to be the actual forger," Alex said. He was watching Morgan, who couldn't quite meet his steady gaze. "Will you give me a straight answer to one question?" he asked her.

"That depends on the question."

"Does Burt have anything to do with these forgeries?"

She said, "He . . . ," but she couldn't finish it.

"Yes," Sarah said flatly, "he does." Why lie or evade the issue?

"How deeply is he involved in this scam?"

"Deeply."

Morgan said, "Sarah, for God's sake . . ."

"Let her talk." He asked Sarah, "Is Burt responsible for the redness and swelling on Morgan's nose?"

"No."

"Because if he is . . ."

"He's not. That's the truth."

"Do you know where he is now?"

"No, we don't. No more questions, Alex, please. Morgan's right, I've said enough for now."

". . . All right. I won't pressure either of you. But I will offer some advice." His eyes were on Morgan again. "I care about you, and I don't want to see you hurt any more than you have been already—no, don't say anything, just listen. Don't keep whatever you know about these forgeries to yourself too long. If you do, and any of this comes out, you could be implicated. Go to the authorities first. Or at least get yourself a good attorney."

"Steps have already been taken," Sarah said.

"Morgan?"

"Yes. You don't need to worry."

"I'll worry anyway, if you don't mind." He gave her a long searching look. "So. These paintings. You're not planning to take them back where you found them?"

"No."

"What, then? Store them somewhere?"

"We hadn't thought that far ahead."

"One thing you'd better not do is take them home with you," he said. "Here's another option—leave them with me for the time being, let me put them in a safe place. Until you decide what you're going to do about them . . . and about Burt."

"I don't know—"

Sarah said, "I think it's a good idea, Morgan."

"Any time you want them," Alex said, "for any reason, just let me know. The same goes if you feel the need to unburden yourselves. I'm a good listener, I'm nonjudgmental, and I don't break confidences."

Sarah believed him. She said as much to Morgan in the car a few minutes later. "He's a good man. And he genuinely cares about you."

"I know. I wish . . ."

"What?"

"Never mind. It doesn't matter."

It did matter. Not at the moment, but potentially. What Morgan wished was that she'd loved and married a man like Alex Hazard instead of Alias. Just as Sarah wished she'd fallen in love with and married a man like David. Too late for Morgan? Probably not, if she had any reciprocal feelings for Alex. Too late for Sarah herself now? Maybe not. Maybe once the alias man was out of her life for good, and the ghost of "Scott" had finally been laid, she could turn to David with an open mind and an open heart and learn to love him.

But first, she and Morgan had to do something else. Before they could even begin to love other men, they had to learn to love themselves, love life again.

Jessie

San Francisco, California

S ERENA was barefoot, dressed in black leotards and a black tank top, her black hair hanging stringily down her back and across one breast as if she hadn't washed it in days. In one hand she held a can of Diet Coke. There was another kind of coke, or some similar chemical substance, inside her: her pupils were dilated to the size of pebbles. She reeked of marijuana, too. Stoned to the max. The blank stare said she didn't know Jessie from Babe the Blue Ox.

"So what're you selling?" she said.

"I'm not selling anything, Serena."

"Hey, you know me? I don't know you."

"I'm Frank Court's friend."

"Who? Oh, sure, Frank."

"We met at Dalishar's home in Santa Fe, remember?"

"Oh, sure, sure," but the stare remained blank.

"Is Frank here?"

"Nobody here but me."

"Have you seen Frank recently?"

"Uh-uh. Just Dalishar. I've about had it with him."

"Why is that?"

"I don't like to be alone. Bored out of my skull, you know?"

"Well, I'm here now. Is it okay if I come in?"

"I'm not supposed to let anybody in. Not supposed to answer the door or the phone."

"You've already answered the door. It's freezing out here, Serena."

"Cold as a witch's tit, this city. Fog every day, gray gray gray. I hate the fog, hate to be cold."

"Let's talk inside then, where it's warm. Just for a few minutes."

"All right, what the hell. You're a friend of Frank's, right?"

"And Dalishar's."

"Fuck Dalishar," Serena said. She opened the door and stepped aside for Jessie to enter.

It wasn't only warm inside the house, it was stifling; heat radiated in palpable shimmers. She must have had the furnace cranked up over eighty. The living room was a mess, as if a small tornado had torn through it—papers and Coke cans and dirty dishes strewn every which way, a chair and a lamp overturned. The only light came from a dozen flickering candles, fat and thin, tall and short. The spicy-sweet scent of incense was heavy—a smell Jessie had never particularly liked, made even more sickening by the feverish atmosphere and by hanging layers of marijuana smoke. An odd, twangy music—Indian sitar?—came from a home entertainment center on one wall.

"What's your name again?" Serena asked.

"Jessie."

"You want a joint, Jessie?"

"No, thanks." She'd have to take shallow breaths to avoid a contact high as it was.

"Can't give you any blow, I only got a couple of lines left."

"No problem. Who told you not to let anybody in or answer the phone?"

Serena sat cross-legged on a bunch of mismatched pillows piled on the floor. She took a prerolled joint out of a plastic tin, lit it, and inhaled deeply before she answered. "Dalishar, who else?"

"Is he coming back soon?"

"Don't ask me."

"When did you see him last?"

"Yesterday? Yeah, yesterday. He blew in for about half an hour, then blew right back out again. Hardly even looked at me."

"Do you know where he went?"

"How'd I know? He doesn't tell me anything."

"How long have you been here?"

"Forever, man. A lifetime."

"One day, two days?"

"Two, three, a goddamn lifetime when you're alone."

"Why don't you leave, go back to Santa Fe?"

"No bread, that's why. None in this dump—I looked."

"What about Ellen Duncombe?"

"Who?"

"The woman who owns the house."

"Oh, yeah, Duncan. What about her?"

"Where is she?"

"Who knows? Who cares?"

"What's her relationship with Dalishar?"

Serena giggled. "It's not sex, that's for sure. She's an old lez."

"Art? Something to do with art?"

"Yeah, that's right, he said that once."

"Said what?"

"She had a school, she was his teacher when he was starting out."

"Is that all he told you about her?"

"All he ever said, yeah."

"What did they talk about when you got here?"

"Huh?"

Patience, patience. "Dalishar and Ellen Duncombe."

"I dunno."

"Did they go away together?"

"Who knows? I didn't come with him. All by myself."

"But Ellen was here, wasn't she?"

"Nobody was here."

"Then how did you get into the house?"

"Key under a flowerpot. He told me where it was."

The incense and marijuana stink was making Jessie light-headed. She sat on the edge of a rocking chair across from the girl. "Let me get this straight. Dalishar called you in Santa Fe two or three days ago and told you to fly to San Francisco and wait for him here, is that it?"

"Yeah. Bus to Albuquerque, bullshit security, boring plane flight, boring taxi ride to this foghole—all by myself. Used up all the money I had."

"Why did he want you to meet him here?"

"Go somewhere afterward, someplace warm. Cabo, maybe. Cabo's a ball, you ever been to Cabo?"

"No. Afterward, you said. After what?"

"Some big deal he's got going."

"What kind of deal?"

Shrug. "Big bucks, he said. Gonna live like royalty. We don't live so damn bad right now, back in Santa Fe. Nice house, parties, plenty of dope, everything you could want."

"Who else was involved?"

"Huh?"

"This deal. Frank? Ellen Duncombe? Both of them?"

Shrug.

"All right," Jessie said. "So then he showed up yesterday, but went right back out again."

"Yeah. I asked him did he want to fuck, he never even looked at me. He always wants to fuck."

"What did he do while he was here?"

"Tore up the place. Weird, man."

"Tore it up. Looking for something, you mean?"

"Yeah, I guess."

"Did he find it?"

"I don't think so. Pissed when he got here, even more pissed when he left. All red in the face and growling like a dog."

"Talking to himself? Do you remember what he said?"

"Hey, I wasn't listening. He didn't want anything to do with me, I didn't want anything to do with him." Serena took a last deep drag, scratched out what was left of the roach. Yawned, burrowed down into the pillows, and closed her eyes. "You sure you don't want a joint?" she said sleepily. "It's good shit, Mexican shit."

"No. But I'd like to use the bathroom."

"Sure, go ahead. You can find it, no problem."

Jessie went through a doorway into a short hall. The bathroom was the first door on the left; she bypassed it and entered the nearest bedroom. Ellen Duncombe's bedroom, from the looks of it. The mattress had been pulled off the bed, drawers yanked out and up-ended, the contents of the closet hurled into a mound that spilled out over the rug. She poked among the scattered contents of the drawers, but it was all mundane personal items.

A second bedroom had been treated in a similar fashion. So had the woman's office or studio, a large room at the rear with a glassed-in back wall. It appeared as though she had once painted here, but not recently: no supplies or works in progress. Two finished oils, one of which bore a resemblance to a Franz Kline Jessie had seen once in a Philadelphia gallery, hung crookedly on the wall. Two others had been ripped down and stomped into shreds. Dalishar on his first destructive rampage yesterday. She hunted through the wreckage, looking for an address book, a Rolodex, any papers that contained names, addresses. Nothing. The only item of interest she found was a framed photograph of an angular, fiftyish woman with short brown hair and a thin-lipped smile, standing in front of a sign that read "Duncombe School of Modern Art." Ellen Duncombe? She slipped the photo out of the frame.

On her way out, the telephone caught her eye—a portable unit, the base still on one corner of a secretary desk, the receiver knocked off to the floor. She picked up the receiver. It was the kind that had to be turned on to answer or make a call; she flipped the switch, heard a dial tone, shut it off again, and set it down on the base.

When she came back into the living room, Serena was still lying supine in her nest of pillows, motionless, eyes shut. The sitar music continued to play, the incense- and pot-laden air seemed even more stifling. Jessie knelt and shook the girl's arm. No response. She did it again with more energy. Serena's eyes popped open in a vacant stare.

"Floating, man," she said.

"Serena, wake up, listen to me."

"Huh? Hoo, I'm really stoned."

Jessie shook her again, kept shaking her until the dilated eyes began to focus. Then she held the color photo close to the girl's face, told her to look at it. Serena squinted at her instead.

"Hey, you still here?"

"Look at the photo, Serena. Is the woman Ellen Duncombe?"

"Duncan? I dunno. . . ."

"Is this Ellen Duncombe?"

". . . Yeah. Damn old lez."

"All right." Jessie slipped the photo into her purse. "Now listen to me and stay focused. Have there been any telephone calls since you've been here?"

"Calls?"

"That's right. Has the phone rung? Have—there—been—any—calls?"

"Yeah, two, three, who knows? What—"

"Did you answer?"

"What?"

"Dalishar told you not to answer the door, but you let me in. He told you not to answer the phone—did you answer the phone?"

"First time, yeah."

"Who was it?"

"Some lez friend of Ellen's . . . gave me a hard time, so I hung up on her."

"You didn't answer the other calls?"

"No. Hell with it, let 'em go on the machine."

"Answering machine?" Jessie said. "Where? I didn't see it."

Vague gesture. "Somewhere in here. . . ."

Jessie found it on a table behind the couch, another portable unit with the red numeral 3 blinking in the message box. The reason she hadn't seen it before was that it was mostly hidden under an afghan. Three messages. She pushed the Play button. The first two messages were from a woman named Linda who sounded angry and demanded to know who the bitch answering Ellen Duncombe's phone was. The third was in a different, coolly businesslike woman's voice—

"This message is for Allan Cooney. Please call Candace Viner as soon as possible, with regard to our business transaction. I have reservations about the Cézanne that need to be resolved before I make the wire transfer."

Allan Cooney. Another "C-o" last name; he was a consistent bastard when it came to his aliases. She looked at the machine's date and time box. The call had come in at 9:45 this morning. Then she replayed the message and copied down the telephone number the caller had left. No area code. Which must mean Candace Viner lived within the same 415 area.

In a drawer under the phone she found a local white pages. There was no San Francisco listing for anyone named Viner. Unlisted number, or else the woman lived in another city within the 415 area code. Jessie checked the 415 prefixes in the front of the book. Yes: Marin County. That was north across the Golden Gate Bridge, if she remembered correctly.

Serena was sitting up now, sipping Diet Coke. Jessie asked her, "Do you know a woman named Candace Viner?"

"Who? Candace?"

"Do you know her?"

"No."

"Is the name familiar?"

"Uh-uh. What kind of name is Candace anyway?"

"She's a friend of Frank's."

"Frank's got lots of friends. You, you're his friend, right?"

Wrong. I'm one of his worst enemies.

"How about a joint? It's good shit, Mexican shit. . . ."

Hopeless.

Did Dalishar know Candace Viner, know where she lived? If so, he'd have gone to see her last night, and there wasn't any hint of that in the message. Even if he had, she didn't know where Alias was, either, as of 9:45 this morning. Maybe she still hadn't been in touch with him.

Maybe there was still time.

Morgan

Los Alegres, California

THEY were in the driveway, just getting out of Sarah's rental car, when the silver-and-blue Outback pulled up in front. Morgan recognized it immediately: Laurel's. Now what did she want?

Laurel hopped out, waved. One of her daughters was with her— Kristen, the chubby, spoiled eight-year-old. Hand in hand, they came skipping up the front walk. That was Laurel, a big kid herself.

"Company," Sarah said, sotto voce.

"Another friend. I'll get rid of her."

Kristen dragged her mother to a stop, prompting Laurel to say, "Don't pull my arm out of the socket, for heaven's sake." She ran her free hand through her rumpled brown hair. Rumpled was the word for her. Rumpled hair, rumpled clothing, movements so loose-jointed they had a rumpled effect. In addition to that, she seldom wore makeup, had a crooked smile and a Lauren Hutton gap between her front teeth—and she still managed to look more attractive than ninety percent of women her age. Morgan had always envied her, the casual beauty and the easy, casual attitude that went with it.

Sarah received a curious once-over, Morgan a look that changed the crooked smile to a frown. "What happened to your nose? It looks a little inflamed."

"An accident. Nothing serious."

"Well, at least you're still among the living. I was beginning to wonder. Don't you listen to your phone messages?"

"I meant to call you. I've been busy."

"Aren't we all. Who's this?"

Morgan introduced Sarah as "an old friend from Vancouver."

"Vancouver? Never mentioned you and Burt knew anyone in Canada. Where is Burt, anyway? On another of his business trips?"

"Yes. Was there something you wanted?"

"An ice cream," Kristen said. "That's what *I* want."

"Hush."

"Mama, you promised. You said if I finished my book report—"

"All right, just be patient." Laurel sighed and rolled her eyes. She said to Morgan, "You didn't listen to my last message," in chiding tones.

"What?"

"Jack and I are having a dinner party Saturday night. We wanted you and Burt to come."

"Oh . . . right."

"Can you make it? Or won't Burt be back by then?"

"No. He won't."

"Well . . . if Sarah's still here on Saturday . . ."

"I won't be," Sarah said.

"That's too bad. Maybe the three of us can get together before you leave? I've heard a lot of good things about Vancouver and British Columbia."

Kristen tugged at her mother's arm. "Mama, Baskin Robbins, please?"

"I'll call you," Morgan said.

"Yes, do that. All right, Kristen, all *right*."

Laurel let the child lead her away. On impulse Morgan followed, drew her to one side as Kristen clambered into the Outback.

"Remember what you told me the last time we talked? About seeing Burt with a woman on Mark West Springs Road?"

Laurel's gaze sideslipped. She said, "Um, sure, but it wasn't Burt. I thought it might be, but it wasn't."

"You don't have to lie to me, Laurel."

"Well . . . even if it was, it doesn't have to mean anything."

"What did the woman look like?"

"I didn't get a very good look at her—"

"Short, dark hair, you said."

"Not really dark, just darker than yours. Light brown."

"How short?"

"Oh, you know, close on her head. Not very stylish."

"How old was she?"

"Older than us. At least forty-five."

"Attractive?"

"Not very. Thin, sort of bony. The severe type. That's why I'm sure there wasn't anything, you know, going on there. It must've been business or something."

"Yes, it must've been."

"Does she sound familiar?"

"No."

"Well." Laurel rumpled her hair. "Morgan . . . it's none of my business, but is everything all right between you and Burt?"

She couldn't bring herself to do any more pretending; it was all going to come out soon enough anyway. "No," she said, "everything is not all right." And never was.

"Oh, God, I'm sorry—"

"Don't be. I'm not anymore."

She left Laurel looking flustered, made herself walk slowly to the porch. She unlocked the door, went in ahead of Sarah—and it was no longer like coming home. The house had a strange feel, familiar and yet unfamiliar, not quite real, like a house in a dream. Illusion. Her whole life here, so apparently normal for nearly four years, had been an illusion. Elaborate hoax, conjuror's trick, monstrous joke.

Sarah gave her a quizzical look as she shut the door. "You look a little pale. Are you all right?"

"I will be."

"What did you ask your friend? Or was it private?"

"No." Morgan told her about the woman Laurel had seen with Alias. "I wanted to get a description of her."

"You're thinking it was the woman at the farm, the one with the Ford."

"Must've been. On a shopping trip, in his car."

"Another member of the forgery ring. One of the artists."

"Probably. The description ought to help identify her."

"Is she still with Alias, do you suppose, wherever he is?"

"Not likely," Morgan said. "Why would he take her with him? She's not a slender blond in her thirties."

"Something to do with his half-million-dollar deal."

"Include her but not Dalishar? That doesn't sound like Alias."

"You're right, it doesn't."

"They must've gone their separate ways. Either that, or—"

"Or what?"

Gooseflesh crawled on her arms. "That blood we found."

"What about it? Are you thinking it's hers?"

"Or his," Morgan said.

Jessie

San Francisco, California

THE woman who answered the phone said, "Hello, the Viner residence," in a pronounced Latin accent. Jessie asked to speak to Candace Viner on a matter of urgent importance, and added in Spanish, "*Muy importante*," to drive the point home. The woman went away. Silence thrummed in Jessie's ears.

It was chilly in the fog-wrapped rental car; she started the engine, put on the heater. Cold air blasted against her legs. The air jets seemed to stay cold for a long time, then grew hot very fast. Too hot. She switched the heater off but left the engine running.

A wary voice said in her ear, "Yes?"

"Candace Viner?"

"Yes, this is she."

"Is Allan Cooney there with you, by any chance?"

Long pause. "No, he's not."

"When did you hear from him last?"

"Who is this, please?"

"My name is Jessie Keene. You don't know me."

"Friend of Allan's? Business associate?"

"Neither. And his name isn't Allan Cooney."

". . . What did you say?"

"His name isn't Allan Cooney. Or Frank Court. Or Scott

Collins. Or Burton Cord. Or any of God knows how many other aliases he's used."

Jessie could hear the low, quick inhale-exhale of Candace Viner's breathing. After several seconds, "Just who are you?"

"A widow from Elton, Pennsylvania, who's trying to save you a lot of grief."

"Yes? Just what is your relationship with . . . Allan?"

"Until he met you, I was intended to be his latest victim."

More breathy silence.

"There are two other victims in the area at present. One in Los Alegres, where he's been living the past four years. Another down from Canada."

"Just what do you mean by victim?"

"Of fraud, marital and financial."

"Fraud?" Sharp intake of breath this time.

"You've made a business deal with him, is that right?"

"And if I have?"

"Involving art. Expensive art. How did he represent himself?"

"As a dealer in fine art."

"Well, he isn't. He's a con man, a serial bigamist, and a thief. Among other things. What did he sell you, besides himself? One or more Cézanne paintings alleged to be worth half a million dollars?"

"How did you—!"

"With the money to be paid by wire transfer, to an overseas or offshore bank account, probably. Have you completed the transfer yet?"

". . . No."

"Good. Then you haven't seen or talked to him today."

"No."

"Has anyone else contacted you about him recently?"

"No."

"Do you know a Santa Fe artist named Dalishar?"

"No." Both coolness and wariness were gone from the woman's voice; it had turned hard and tight with each successive negative. Whoever Candace Viner was, she was neither stupid nor a shrinking violet. "Where are you calling from, Mrs. Keene?"

"San Francisco."

"Are you willing to come to my home, discuss this matter in person?"

"Absolutely. The sooner the better."

"With proof of what you've just told me?"

"Enough proof to satisfy you that it's the truth."

"I live in Ross," Candace Viner said. Hard as nails now. "Ridgeway Road in Ross. Do you know where that is?"

"Somewhere in Marin County."

"You'll need directions." She gave them in clipped sentences; Jessie wrote them down. "I'll expect you in an hour," she said, and broke the connection.

✦

Jessie was on Park Presidio Drive, on her way to the Golden Gate Bridge, when her cell phone burred. She pawed it out of her purse.

Morgan.

With more news, even bigger news than hers.

✦

Art forgery.

Well, of course. It had to be something like that. Alias, with an interest in art and years of experience at running scams; Dalishar, an unsuccessful artist with expensive tastes; Ellen Duncombe, another artist whose skills were imitative. An unholy trio: Ellen Duncombe painting most of the fakes, Dalishar using his minor reputation in the art world to locate likely buyers among dealers and collectors in the West and Southwest, Alias arranging for a quiet, out-of-the-way forgery studio and putting together seller's packages and brokering the phonies. It must have been a thriving but small-scale operation until recently. Then Alias had made contact with Candace Viner, a woman obviously interested in fine art, obviously rich, and obviously susceptible to his special brand of charm. Somehow he'd convinced her to pay half a million dollars for one or more fakes on bogus proof of authenticity—the deal of a lifetime, a con man's dream score. And in his greed and conceit, he'd determined not to share it with his two partners. Take the money and run.

Except that things hadn't gone quite as planned. For some reason Candace Viner had become suspicious enough to hold off on the wire transfer. And within the past couple of days Dalishar had gotten wind of the double-cross and come hunting him.

Clear enough, up to that point. But so much still wasn't clear. Where was Alias? Why hadn't he tried to liberate his stash of money from the safe deposit box? Why hadn't he checked on the wire transfer and contacted Candace Viner to find out why it hadn't gone through? Where was Dalishar? Where was Ellen Duncombe?

Still, the important thing, as Jessie said to Morgan, then in a call to Harvey Blakiston, was this: Wherever Alias was, he hadn't gotten his hands on the half million dollars. And wouldn't, now. The sixty-four thousand in cash and his phony passports were also beyond his reach. He couldn't run very far or very long without money and with an ever-growing list of people working together to bring him down. His luck was running out.

Sarah

Los Alegres, California

THERE was nothing to do now but wait for Jessie. Neither she nor Morgan felt like eating. The thought of a Scotch crossed Sarah's mind, but the desire was fleeting; she didn't want a drink more than she wanted a drink. All to the good. Alcohol had been a crutch for too long, a painkiller that only created more pain. It was time, past time, she learned to walk again without it.

Right now what she wanted most was a little time alone. Morgan seemed to feel the same way. As close as they'd become in such a short time, it was more a business partnership than a friendship, and they each needed space, breathing room. Private time for private reflection, a little private suffering. When they met with Jessie for the first time in an hour or two, there would be plenty to discuss. Until then, there seemed little left to say to each other.

Morgan retreated to the side porch. And Sarah wandered out into the back yard, drawn by the warmth of the sunshine.

The yard was large, dominated by two shade trees and a well-kept lawn bordered by flower beds. Rhododendrons grew in shady patches along the property fences. Pleasant. Not unlike her garden at the Kitsilano house . . . in that other life she'd led. Alias's hand here, too? Probably. He'd never been much of a gardener himself, but he'd been a font of suggestions, and of course she had followed them all. To make him happy. Such a good little doting wife she'd been.

Under a sprawling liquidambar tree was a grouping of outdoor furniture. Sarah drew one of the chaise longues out of the shade into the light, sat with her face upturned to the sun. She knew she should put on sun block—Morgan probably had some—but it was too much of a bother. The dim prospect of skin cancer was the least of her worries.

The heat was cleansing. It warmed her body, burned away some of the tension, purged her mind for the first time in days. Long minutes passed without thought—time spent in an effulgent vacuum. But of course it didn't last. She wasn't used to direct sun; it brought prickly sweat and discomfort along with returning awareness. All on the surface anyway. Baked on the outside, still raw and frozen on the inside.

She dragged the chaise longue back into the shade. Sat there cooling and allowing herself to think again . . . think too much. Alias. Morgan, Jessie. Alias. Dalishar, Ellen Duncombe, forged artworks, half a million dollars, Alex Hazard. Alias Alias Alias . . .

Home, the bookshop.

David.

A vague guilt stirred in her. Those messages yesterday—and more today, no doubt. Worried about her because she'd vanished so suddenly, without telling him or anyone else that she was going away. Worried because he cared about her. And no matter to him that it was completely one-sided, had always been completely one-sided. She'd not been a true friend, for God's sake, not even a decent one. Used him, that was all. Used his attention, his caring, his body, his money . . . all for her own selfish needs. A taker, never a giver. Even when she let him sleep with her, she'd given him nothing of herself. Whore. Worse, an emotional vampire.

She pushed off the chaise longue, went into the house. Hushed in there; whatever Morgan was doing, she made no sounds. Sarah found her purse, rummaged inside. Her fingers touched the little .32 automatic, jerked away from its cold, slick surface. Truth: She didn't like guns any more than Morgan did. She could shoot well enough, thanks to Alias, but what she'd told Morgan might have been false bravado, a lie. Maybe she could actually shoot somebody in self-defense . . . and maybe she couldn't.

Alias? The thought made her shiver. Pray to God she was never put in a position where she had to find out.

Her cell phone was at the bottom of the bag; she took it back outside. The least she could do for David right now was to let him know she was all right. No explanations yet, not on the phone. Too soon for unburdening, confession; and when the time came, she would do it in person. She owed him that much.

Four messages, all brief and all from David. But they weren't quite what she'd expected. In three of them he said, "Please call me as soon as you can. I need to talk to you about something important, very important." Lord, now what? It was after three o'clock; unless he had a court date, he should still be in his office. She tapped out the number, spoke to his secretary, and yes, he was there. He came on the line immediately.

"Sarah, this is a relief. I was really starting to worry."

"I know, I'm sorry. I only just picked up your messages."

"Bright Lights closed, no sign of you at home . . . where did you go so suddenly?"

"Out of town for a few days. I needed to get away."

"Out of town where? Where are you?"

She almost told a lie, to circumvent questions, but there had been enough lies in her life. Too many lies. She said, "California."

Short, heavy silence. "Where in California?"

"Does it matter? I'll be home in a few days . . ."

"Sarah—where in California?"

"A small town north of San Francisco. Los Alegres."

"Oh, my God," he said. He sounded stricken. "You know."

". . . Know what?"

"About Scott, the truth about Scott."

All at once, she was cold again. "What truth, David?"

"You wouldn't have gone there, of all places, if you hadn't found out—"

"What truth? Say it."

"That he's still alive, married to somebody else . . ."

I know more than that now, a whole lot more.

"Sarah? How did you find out?"

"How did *you* find out? You tell me first."

"All right . . . that's why I've been calling you, I wanted to break the news myself in person, soften the blow—"

"Tell me how."

"Not like this, long distance. It won't sound right—"

Cold, and angry too, now. Thin, cold anger. "How, dammit?"

"You've been so miserable lately, getting worse all the time. . . . I couldn't stand it any longer. I thought . . . some kind of closure . . . No, that's not really true. I didn't believe it from the first . . ."

"You're not making sense."

She heard him draw a ragged breath. "I never quite believed he died on the island four years ago. The abandoned car in a remote place like Tofino—the whole business seemed contrived, false. I wish I'd been honest with you. I never liked the man, I never trusted him."

"What did you do?"

"Hired a detective agency to find out if he was still alive. Not just once—two different agencies, years apart."

"I see."

"The first one a month or so after he disappeared. They couldn't find a trace of him. I thought I must be wrong, convinced myself it didn't really matter, you'd get over him in time. But you didn't, you just kept grieving. Two months ago—another agency in Seattle. Grabbing at straws. I was half crazy with worry about you, I didn't know what else to do. Sarah, please understand. I did it for you."

Too many lies! "Liar," she said. "You did it for yourself."

"No. I love you, you know that, but—"

"I don't know anything anymore."

"The truth—I know how much it must hurt, but in the long run . . ."

She didn't answer.

"Have you seen him yet? Talked to him?"

"No."

"Good. I don't think you should, alone. Why don't I fly down there—"

"No!"

"You need somebody—"

"I don't need you. Not here. Not anywhere."

"Oh, Christ, I was afraid of this—"

"How long have you known he was alive?"

"Only two days. The report came yesterday morning."

"What else did it say about him? His real name, his background?"

"They weren't able to trace him backward, just forward. It's as if he never existed before you met him at the art exhibit here. Pure blind luck they managed to follow a cold trail to that town in California . . . they turned up a retired fisherman who gave him a ride from Tofino that day—"

"I don't care about that," she said. "Those details don't interest me."

"Sarah . . . I don't understand how you could have found out. How? When?"

"I've known since Monday night," she said. "I would have known Friday night, if I'd had five thousand dollars. But I had to wait until I could get it from you."

". . . That's what you needed the loan for?"

"To buy the same information you bought."

"Five thousand dollars? That's an extortionate figure."

"I'd have paid twice as much. Lied to you to get twice as much."

"You didn't need to lie. I wish to God you hadn't."

"So do I. Now."

"Who did you pay the money to?"

"I don't know. He wouldn't tell me his name."

"How'd he get in touch with you?"

"Called me at the bookshop Friday night."

"Where did he get the information?"

"I don't know."

"You met him in person? What did he look like?"

"After nightfall in Stanley Park. I never saw his face."

"It has to be somebody from the agency in Seattle," David said grimly. "One of their field operatives . . . one goddamn rotten apple. Whoever he is, he'll regret it. I'll make certain of that."

"I'm sure you will. If you can get the money back, then I won't owe you anything."

"I don't care about the money, I care about you. If you'd only confided in me—"

"I could say the same thing, couldn't I?"

"I thought I was doing the right thing," he said. "I still think so. Now that you know the truth about Scott or whatever his real name is, maybe—"

"Maybe what?"

"You'll stop pining away for him, stop putting your life on hold."

"And start living it with you?"

"Whether you believe it or not, that wasn't—isn't—my primary motive. I'd like us to be together, I ache for it, but if your future doesn't include me, all right, as long as you're well again."

"Very noble, David."

"I mean it." There was a small silence before he said, "You're not still in love with him, even now? After what he did to you?"

"No. I'm not in love with him anymore."

"Once you see him . . . you are going to see him?"

"Oh, yes. Sooner or later."

"And then? What'll you do about him?"

"I don't know yet."

"You could have him arrested. Bigamy, desertion . . ."

"Minor charges," she said, "minor sins. He's guilty of worse crimes than those, worse crimes and worse sins."

"I don't . . . what are you talking about?"

"Topics for another time and another place. Good-bye for now, David."

"Wait, don't hang up. How can I get in touch—"

She hung up. And switched off the phone so he couldn't call back.

For a while she sat unmoving, her thoughts switched off as well—temporary shutdown for repairs. From somewhere not far off a leafblower began its querulous whine; the sudden noise brought her out of herself.

Damn fool, she thought then. Damn fool!

And she wasn't sure if she meant David or herself.

Jessie

Ross, California

Ross turned out to be a pocket of suburban wealth some twenty miles northwest of San Francisco—large homes on spacious, tree-shaded lots, and higher up in the low rolling hills, gated and walled estates of several acres each. Candace Viner's address was one of the estates, her home a modernistic redwood-and-glass pile behind a short entrance drive that curled through a stand of pine. Formal gardens were on one side, a garage and what looked like a guest house on the other, and no doubt a swimming pool hidden at the rear. Parked in the crushed-shell circle in front were a new Cadillac and a bright red Ferrari.

The trappings of wealth had never impressed Jessie. What did impress her, once she got inside the house, was the amount and diversity of artwork on display—sculptures in wood, iron, and crystal, and large and small paintings and lithographs by a variety of Impressionists, Postimpressionists, and modern realists. That, and Candace Viner.

The woman was waiting for her in a formal living room whose glass rear wall overlooked a broad terrace and the expected swimming pool. For one thing, she was a striking green-eyed redhead, early forties, tanned and toned in a beige linen business suit, a diamond wedding ring on one hand that must have been at least three carats and other expensive jewelry at her wrists and throat.

The aura she projected, aside from that of wealth, was one of cool, businesslike self-absorption. For another thing, she'd brought in a third party to audit the meeting. At first Jessie thought the tall, gray-haired, fiftyish man in the three-piece suit was her husband. Wrong guess.

"This is my attorney, Charles Haldane. You have no objection to his being present, I trust?"

"None at all."

Haldane said, "Or to having our discussion recorded?"

"Same answer."

He produced a voice-activated pocket recorder and switched it on. "Identification and references first, please."

Jessie provided her name, address, and pedigree, the same for John Dollarhide and Harvey Blakiston, and a handful of other references in Elton, Philadelphia, and New York. Then she gave them a no-holds-barred account of Alias's fraudulent marital and art-related activities, as much information as she and Morgan and Sarah had gathered to date. Neither Candace Viner nor her lawyer had anything to say until she was finished. The woman's expression revealed nothing of what she was thinking. Haldane's showed a balancing act between acceptance and skepticism.

"That's rather a fantastic story," he said.

"The truth is often fantastic. And in this case, easily verifiable."

"Perhaps. Just what is it you expect to gain, Mrs. Keene?"

"Gain?"

"From contacting Mrs. Viner as you have?"

"I told you. To keep her from completing the wire transfer of funds to Alias's account. He no longer has access to the cash in his private safe deposit box. He can't run very far, or hide very long, without funds."

"And that's your only motive?"

"No. When he's caught and brought to trial, I'd like Mrs. Viner to join me and his other victims in testifying against him. All of us together can put him away for a good long time."

Haldane still wasn't convinced. He said, "Candace?"

She didn't reply. In fact, she ignored him completely. Her eyes, as they had been the entire time, were on Jessie—a steady, probing, analytical gaze. At length she said, "You did say you were a widow, Mrs. Keene?"

"That's right."

"Something else we have in common. How long?"

"Seven months."

"And how long were you married?"

"Seventeen years."

"Do you mind telling me how old your husband was?"

"Forty-three. Congenital heart disease."

"Jordan died thirteen months ago, at the age of seventy-six," Candace Viner said. "We were married when I was twenty-two and he was fifty-five. I was his third wife—his trophy wife."

She said the last matter-of-factly, without apology. Haldane flashed her a faintly disapproving look; she ignored that, too. Outspoken as well as self-absorbed, Jessie thought, a woman who didn't much care what people thought of her or her motives. Point in her favor.

"Despite the difference in our ages, we were happy and good to and for each other. He was a brilliant and fascinating man. Self-made—he held sixteen industrial engineering patents. What was your husband's profession?"

"Advertising."

"And your marriage was also a happy one, I'm sure."

"Very."

"Candace," Haldane said, "I think we're straying from the point here . . ."

"Do you?" To Jessie she said, "One of Jordan's passions was fine art, and it became mine as well. He taught me to understand and appreciate all types of art. Our tastes were similar in some things, but they differed considerably in other areas. Oils and watercolors, for one. He preferred abstract art and nudes of all types, from the sublime to the erotic. I prefer the Impressionists and Postimpressionists, particularly the French—Seurat, Monet, Matisse, Cézanne, Renoir. Since Jordan's death, I've added a few originals to Jordan's collection, but nothing major, nothing truly unusual. I suppose you could say I was hungry. Or perhaps ripe is a better word."

"How long ago did you meet Allan Cooney?"

"A month or so."

"Museum, gallery, art exhibit?"

"A gallery on Post Street in the city."

"And he claimed to be an art dealer?"

"Yes. From Chicago. Specializing in obscure and previously unknown works by established artists. His credentials seemed impeccable, and he was quite charming. So impeccable and so charming that I didn't find it necessary to check on their authenticity."

"I wish you'd come to me before you made any deals with the man," Haldane said. "I would certainly have advised you to—"

"I don't need you to berate me, Charles. I have been doing a more than adequate job of berating myself."

"I didn't mean to embarrass you."

"Didn't you?" Candace Viner dismissed him again, said to Jessie, "We struck up a conversation. Or rather, now that I've had occasion to think about it, he struck up a conversation with me. Later we went out for coffee and a discussion of art. He was quite knowledgeable, though his taste differed markedly from mine."

"His being a passion for the macabre and outré," Jessie said. "Goya's 'black paintings,' Bosch, that sort of thing."

"You do know him well, don't you."

"Too well. Did he try to sell you anything at that first meeting?"

"No. But I told him I am always interested in acquiring new paintings, and I foolishly intimated that I was willing to pay dear for rare pieces. He said he would let me know if anything in my area of interest turned up, and we exchanged cards. I expected never to hear from him again."

"Do you still have the card he gave you?"

"Yes. It has a Chicago address and telephone number."

"Mail drop and answering service, probably."

"In any event, I didn't try to contact him. He called me about a week ago. He said he'd come into possession of a Seurat, a Matisse still life, and two early Cézannes, one a brilliant rendering of the forest of Fontainebleu—all previously unknown, all recently discovered in a small private collection in Europe."

"And all resembling known works, but differing in form and subject matter."

"Yes. Completely authenticated, he said, by European experts in the work of each artist. Well, naturally I was quite excited. What serious collector wouldn't be? I invited him to bring the paintings here so I could examine them. He agreed, but he could only bring two, he said, the Seurat and the smaller of the Cézannes. The other two were large and not as easily transported, and he didn't want to move them until a deal had tentatively been struck. But of course he had photographs of those and letters of provenance for all."

Candace Viner stood and took a restless turn around the room, stopped before a tiny framed painting hung in a wall nook. "This is the Seurat," she said. "I was enthralled when I saw it. Seurat has always been one of my favorites, and thanks to Jordan's tutelage, I consider myself something of an expert on his work. This one . . . I would have sworn it was authentic. The dense pointillist technique is quite difficult to imitate. It pains me deeply that it's evidently a forgery, and that I didn't learn my lessons as well as I thought I had."

"Did you have anyone else look at it?" Jessie asked.

"A man whose judgment I trust, yes. The owner of the Post Street gallery I mentioned before. He also believed it—and the first Cézanne—to be authentic, though I admit he advised me to seek other opinions and proceed with caution."

Haldane said mildly, "Why didn't you take the advice?"

Again she ignored him. "Even when Alias, as you call him, named his price for the four paintings, I wasn't suspicious. The figure was quite fair for such rare pieces, if they were genuine."

"Half a million dollars," Jessie said.

"Yes."

Haldane was shocked; his client apparently hadn't mentioned the figure to him before. "Good Lord, Candace," he said.

"Well? I can afford to indulge myself, can't I?"

"Afford to, yes, but five hundred thousand dollars—"

"I didn't make the decision lightly, Charles. Or immediately. I insisted on examining the Matisse and the Cézanne Fountainebleu first, of course, and even after they arrived and the gallery owner and I had both studied them, I spent one full day haggling with Cooney and another making a final decision."

Jessie said, "So the two of you spent quite a bit of time together the past week or so."

"As a matter of fact, he was a guest here during the negotiations."

Haldane disapproved of that, too. "You took him into your home?"

"Into my home, not my bed. I didn't sleep with the man."

"Candace, please—"

"Oh, don't be so damned tight-assed. He wasn't my type, and I don't suppose I was his. It was strictly a business arrangement."

"You completed the deal when?" Jessie asked.

"Yesterday morning. I agreed to wire the money to his account in the Cayman Islands. He wanted it done that way for tax reasons, he said. Yes, yes, Charles, I know it's not strictly aboveboard, but I didn't question it because I'd have done the same if I were the recipient of that much cash. You know well enough how I feel about bloody taxes."

"He left all of the paintings with you?"

"Yes. We 'trusted' each other."

"But you didn't wire the money. A reservation about one of the Cézannes, was it?"

"A flaw I should have noticed earlier and didn't," Candace Viner said. "His work is geometric, somewhere between simple representation and pure abstraction, and the patterned strokes of pigment in one of the sections of trees and houses seemed a bit off somehow, not quite true. I had the gallery owner come in for another look. He'd missed the false note the first time, just as I had. We agreed that it could be nothing more than a simple error in technique, but he suggested again that I call in a Cézanne expert before completing the transaction. This time I listened to him. Allan—Alias—had given me a local number where he could be reached in an emergency, and I called it and left a message—the message you overheard, Mrs. Keene."

"And you've heard nothing from him since yesterday morning?"

"Not a word. Given what you've told me about him, it seems out of character for him to assume the transfer had been made without checking to make sure."

"So it is. And if he had checked, or if he'd gotten your message, he'd certainly have contacted you by now."

"Do you think something's happened to him?"

"Either that, or circumstances have forced him into a radical change of plans."

"What sort of circumstances?" Haldane asked.

"No idea," Jessie said, "unless it has to do with thieves falling out."

"His partners in this forgery ring? This man Dalishar?"

"Most likely."

"Then I think it's time the authorities were notified," Candace Viner said. "Do you agree, Mrs. Keene?"

"I do. The Federal Bureau of Investigation. But before we do anything, I'll want to consult with John Dollarhide again. And with Morgan and Sarah."

"Of course. Charles and I will want to talk to your attorney as well."

"How far are you prepared to go, Mrs. Viner? Are you willing to testify against him in court?"

"Yes. I want this man put out of commission as much as you do."

Haldane said, "You realize what testifying means? The media will have a field day. It could be very embarrassing—"

"I don't care about that. When it comes to public opinion, my skin is as thick as an elephant's."

"Well, it's your decision, of course."

"How clever of you to point that out. My decision, and I've already made it." Wryly, she added, "It seems I'm one of the sisterhood now."

"Sisterhood?"

"Of the women Alias has duped," Jessie said. "Duped, treated with scorn and contempt, humiliated."

Candace Viner's smile was an icy rictus. "Hell hath no fury," she said.

Morgan

Sonoma County, California

THE first face-to-face meeting with Jessie had a curiously schizoid quality. Three lookalike strangers, bound together by nothing more than a single dark thread, and yet in an undefinable way it had some of the feel of a reunion of old if casual friends. Tentative at first, but without awkwardness or strain. The sisterhood, Candace Viner had called them. Sarah said wryly that she preferred the Last Wives Club. Morgan's suggestion was only half-facetious: The three witches from *Macbeth*. Toil and trouble, fire burn and cauldron bubble.

"Yes," Jessie said to that, "and what's cooking in the pot is Alias's skinny ass."

They didn't waste any time at the house. Ten minutes after Jessie's arrival, they were in Sarah's rental car and on their way to Coyote Springs Road. Nearly five o'clock by then, and none of them had any desire to be at that isolated farm after nightfall.

On the way they exchanged information in greater detail. Jessie showed them a photograph of Ellen Duncombe she'd taken from the woman's house in San Francisco, and the image matched Laurel's description of Alias's passenger at the Mark West shopping center. One fact confirmed. Another was that they now knew where Alias had spent the weekend and the early part of this week, and why he hadn't come back for his things or as yet tried to empty his safe deposit box: He'd been too busy putting the finishing touches on his big score.

"But we still don't know where he went after he left Candace Viner's home," Sarah said. "Or why he's been out of touch since."

"Or where he is now," Morgan said.

"I almost hope he's at the farm this time."

"I don't."

"If he is, we'll deal with him," Jessie said. The trip was necessary in any case. She had spoken to John Dollarhide on the way up from Ross, she'd told them, and he'd suggested they liberate as many of the other fakes as they could carry away. The more evidence presented to the FBI, the more inclined they'd be to take immediate action.

"The next time I lay eyes on him, I'd rather it be through prison bars."

"Soon, if he contacts Candace Viner before we go to the FBI tomorrow morning. In that case she'll stall him and arrange an early-afternoon meeting at her home, and agents will be there to arrest him when he shows up. Best-case scenario."

"I don't suppose they'd allow us to be there, too," Sarah said.

"They might, under the circumstances."

Morgan said, "I can think of a couple of worst-case scenarios."

"You mean if he doesn't contact Candace, he might manage to slip away and disappear again?"

"If he hasn't already. Then they might never catch him."

"He can't hide for long with an FBI fugitive warrant out on him. And he can't leave the country without funds and those phony passports of his."

"He could have other money, other passports hidden somewhere. He's so damned clever and slippery."

"He won't get away this time," Sarah said. "He's going to prison where he belongs."

"Unless he's already gone straight to hell."

Jessie said, "Dead? What makes you think he might be dead?"

"I keep remembering the blood Sarah and I found—it could be his."

"I don't believe it."

"Neither do I," Sarah said. "If he is dead, no matter what the reason, it means we've been cheated again. We deserve better justice than that."

Morgan said, "I wish I still believed in a just world."

"I do," Jessie said. "I have to, if I'm going to keep on living in it."

"I think maybe I do too," Sarah said. "He's alive, Morgan. He's alive and we're going to put him in prison. Believe it."

They were right, both of them. She had to believe—that he was alive, that he was going to prison, that the world *was* a just place. If it wasn't, then how could she go on living in it? She couldn't. And that was the most frightening prospect of all.

If she couldn't—then maybe she wouldn't.

✦

The farm was deserted.

But somebody had been there since morning, spent at least a couple of hours on the property. They found that out as soon as they entered the cinder-block building.

"We seem to've been playing tag with one of them," Sarah said. "But which one?"

The remaining paintings were gone, forgeries and framed junkshop art alike. The easels, all the paints and brushes and other supplies, the prints and lithographs, the dropcloths—gone. The squarish interior was empty except for the three tables and the clay-spattered workbench. And the bloodstain near the far window; it hadn't been touched.

"Alias," Jessie said.

"Or Ellen Duncombe. Or even Dalishar."

"Either of them might want the forgeries, but why would they bother with the rest of it?"

"Planning to set up shop somewhere else," Morgan said.

But that wasn't the explanation. Outside, at the rear of the building, they discovered a scatter of wood pieces and two big metal drums that had been used as incinerators. The wood was what was left of the easels and junkshop frames, hammer-broken into fragments. Ashes, still warm beneath the surface, filled both drums. Sarah hunted up a stick, stirred through one of them until she turned up a few remnants of scorched canvas, one clean, the others with bubbles of paint adhering to them.

"All the paintings destroyed, from the way it looks," she said. "New and old, lithographs and prints, even the empty canvases.

The dropcloths were too big to burn; they must have been taken away along with the painting supplies."

Jessie said, "Alias cleaning up after himself."

"Or Dalishar in another of his destructive fits."

"No. He wouldn't take the time; all he cares about is his share of half a million dollars. There wasn't anything here to incriminate him. Or to incriminate Ellen Duncombe. It has to be Alias. He's the one who leased the farm, and he's too smart, too careful, to leave evidence behind that would tie him to a forgery ring."

"If he noticed some of the fakes were missing," Morgan said, "he might suspect I was the one who took them."

"Well, he certainly noticed the broken lock on the door," Sarah said, "but the padlock wasn't damaged. Dalishar must have a key—Alias would think he was responsible, that he broke in in a rage. He wouldn't have any reason to think it was you."

"He would if he's finally tried to get into his safe deposit box."

Jessie said, "Does he know or suspect Dalishar is stalking him? If so, why did it take him so long to clean up here? Why didn't he do it sooner—yesterday?"

"Unable to, for some reason. Avoiding Dalishar, maybe."

"Either that," Sarah said, "or he had something else to clean up first."

"You mean Ellen Duncombe's clothing and car?"

"And maybe Ellen Duncombe herself."

The late-afternoon breeze was chilly on Morgan's neck. "Her blood, then. And Alias killed her. That's almost as bad."

Jessie said, "He's a despicable human being, but a cold-blooded murderer?"

"It may not have been murder," Sarah said. "Some kind of argument that led to violence. Or an accident. And he couldn't leave the body here—it would point straight to him when it was discovered. He'd have to get rid of it somewhere. Get rid of her car and her belongings, too. All that would've taken time, a lot of time. First priority, before he did anything about the paintings."

"It makes sense," Jessie agreed, "and explains a lot of things. Why he didn't check on the wire transfer, why he stayed away from Ellen Duncombe's house in San Francisco, why he hasn't tried to empty his safe deposit box and head for someplace far away from here."

"If you're right," Morgan said, "he will check, and he will try now. If he hasn't already."

"And that means we're going to have to be twice as careful until we talk to the FBI. Spend the night in a hotel. Not up here, in San Francisco. We've been lucky so far, all of us, Alias included. We'd better make sure it's his luck that runs out first."

✦

It was dark by the time they returned to Los Alegres. Morgan suggested, as a precaution, that Sarah drive past her house before stopping. She hadn't left the porch light on, or any lights inside; it should be completely dark. It was. And the driveway and the curb in front were empty.

At the next intersection, Sarah made a U-turn, came back, and parked in front. Ten minutes or so inside, just long enough to gather Sarah's suitcase and for Morgan to toss a few things into an overnight bag, and they'd be on their way to the city. Jessie went in with them to help.

For Morgan, the house still had that same strange, almost surreal feel. And something else, a heaviness in the air, an almost preternatural stillness. Imagination? She stopped in the hallway, reaching for the wall switch.

Before she touched it, a burst of light cut away the shadows in the living room. From where Morgan stood, she could see in through the archway. The light came from the floor lamp next to Alias's favorite chair. And in the chair, waiting, relaxed, one leg crossed over the other—

Her stomach cramped, the same violent sensation as during the worst of her periods. She tasted the bile flavor of fear and disgust.

Him.

Alias.

Sarah

Los Alegres, California

E'D been waiting there in the dark like a spider at the center of one of its webs.

Waiting for Morgan, only Morgan, because when he saw Sarah and Jessie, the relaxed pose vanished; his hands flattened on the chair arms, his body tensed forward, and the mask of poised calm slipped. For two or three seconds she saw what lay beneath the facade, the naked, soulless ego and the icy hatred and the cold calculation and the lust for self-preservation. Then the mask was back in place. He formed a smile with it, wry and rubbery, as he leaned back and recrossed his legs.

"Well," he said. "So this is what's been going on."

Morgan moved into the living room, Sarah and Jessie on either side of her. He looked from one to another of them, showing no expression except for the false smile. He'd changed very little in four years, Sarah thought. A touch of gray at the temples of that beautiful wavy hair, that was all. Still the same lean, hard body. Still the same ascetic face, with its sharp cheekbones, the laugh lines around the wide mouth, the gentle brown eyes. The face she'd fallen in love with, kissed, caressed, adored, pined away for, almost destroyed herself over. A great surge of warmth coursed through her, a powerful feeling composed of equal parts of revulsion and joy, so intense that a bubble of laughter rose and was stillborn in her throat.

The face meant nothing to her anymore. It really was a mask, like one of those Nixon masks kids wore at Halloween—a representation of a human face, as false as the fixed smile, as much of an alias as Scott Collins or Burton Cord or Frank Court or any of the rest of the names he'd used. She knew what lay behind it now, she'd just had a glimpse of the thing that lived in the lean body and wore the handsome face, and it sickened her. And because that was all she felt, now that she'd seen him again, it meant that the ghost had finally been laid, and she was free of him at last.

"You've changed, Sarah," he said. "Still lovely, but thinner, more gaunt than I remember you."

She matched his empty smile and made no reply.

"I don't know if I'm more surprised to see you or Jessie. How have you been, Jessie? Did you receive the flowers I sent?"

"I let them wither and then burned them."

"Pity. Morgan? You don't seem very happy to see me, either."

She didn't reply. Her stride stiff and deliberate, she walked to where he was sitting. "Stand up," she said then.

For a few seconds he looked up at her, smiling. Then he shrugged and lifted slowly to his feet. As soon as he was upright, she slapped him—a roundhouse slap with considerable force behind it, the collision of flesh against flesh making a sound like a whip crack. It rocked him, nearly staggered him.

Sarah tensed. Jessie took a step forward. If he'd retaliated, they would have been all over him like spitting cats. But he didn't. He stood with his arms flat against his sides, his eyes still mild, the smile still in place but crooked now, as if the blow had put a dent in that part of the mask.

"Feel better now?" he said.

"Yes." Morgan raised her hand again.

"Don't. One is all you get."

Jessie said warningly, "Morgan."

It wasn't necessary. She slapped him with words this time— "Fuck you," she said, drawing out both syllables—before she backed away.

"Slaps and foul language," he said. "That's not like you, sweet. You've changed."

"We've all changed," Sarah said. "You changed us."

"Did I?"

"We're not your trusting blond clones any longer. Not credulous. Not weak."

"Not loving, either, obviously. That makes me sad."

"Bullshit."

"I loved you, all three of you, whether you believe it or not. I still do."

"We don't believe it," Jessie said. "None of us ever meant anything to you. We're not women to you, not even human beings. Just things to be used and discarded. Cash cows and sexual playmates."

"That's not true. Would I have stayed with Sarah, with Morgan, as long as I did if I had no feelings for them?"

"Staying was part of the game," Morgan said. "Don't you suppose we've figured that out by now?"

"What game?" Bland innocence, manufactured by the thing behind the lying eyes.

"Power, manipulation, control. You loved every minute of it, got off on it—that's why you stayed. And when you finished emptying our bank accounts and got bored enough or met your next victim, then you moved on. Did you fake your death every time? Is that how you'd've left me if I hadn't challenged you?"

He sighed. "You make me sound like a pretty terrible person."

"That's exactly what you are. You know it, and we know it. Why bother to lie, with the three of us standing here in front of you?"

"You want me to admit that I'm a bigamist? All right, I admit it. A bigamist and a moral coward. But I never meant to hurt any of you. While I was with you, I gave you the best of myself, always."

You never quit, do you? Sarah thought. God, you make me want to puke.

"Was it your doing, bringing Sarah and Jessie here?" he asked Morgan.

"What does it matter?"

"I'd like to know. How did you find out about them?"

"The same way I found out about Doris in Minneapolis and Maureen in Shreveport and Jane in Chicago."

"Ah, I thought so. Have you contacted them, too?"

"Not yet. Soon enough."

"The spare key in my desk, right? Foolish of me to leave it there. But I don't see how you managed to get into the box."

"I found a way."

"Obviously. And now it's empty."

"And that's why you're here," Jessie said.

His gaze held on Morgan. "What did you do with the contents?"

"Contents. Be specific, why don't you. Sixty-four thousand dollars and three phony passports and the photos and the farm lease and the itemized victims' list."

"What did you do with them?"

"You'll never find out."

"Don't be too sure of that," he said. "Who else knows about all of this? The police?"

"The FBI," Sarah said.

Glint of fear in his eyes. She widened her smile when she saw it.

"Nonsense," he said. "Bigamy isn't a federal crime."

"It is in fraud cases where state lines and an international border are crossed."

"There's no proof of fraud in any of my . . . relationships. Even if you brought charges, I'd never be prosecuted. Insufficient evidence."

"There's plenty of evidence of your other crimes."

"What other crimes?"

"Art forgery. Art fraud."

That sliced a deeper rent in the calm facade. His body seemed to harden; a muscle jumped on one cheek. He managed to hold the mask in place, but the smile was gone, and he didn't bother to replace it. Watching, Sarah felt another surge of warmth. Getting to him now, melting some of that icy control.

"So you've been to the farm," he said.

"More than once in the past two days," Morgan said.

Sarah said, "Playing tag with you and Dalishar."

"Dalishar? What do you know about him?"

"We know that he's after you for double-crossing him."

"With blood in his eye," Jessie said.

"How do you know that? You've seen him?"

Morgan said, "Oh, yes, we've seen him."

"Where?"

"Right here in this house."

"I don't believe you. Who else have you seen?"

"You mean at the farm yesterday? Before you cleaned up?"

"What do you mean, cleaned up?"

"What do you think we mean?"

"Don't play games with me."

"Ellen Duncombe," Jessie said.

"I don't know anybody by that name."

"Of course you do. Your other partner in the art scam. The artist who painted most of the fakes."

"And you killed her," Sarah said.

Hard stare. "I've never killed anyone."

"She's dead, isn't she? We found the blood. We know you took her body and her car and hid them somewhere."

"I've never killed anyone," he said again. "There's nothing to tie Ellen Duncombe to me. Nothing to tie me to those paintings, either, not anymore."

"You didn't burn all of them," Morgan said. "We took several and put them in a safe place."

"That doesn't matter. You could have gotten them anywhere. Your word against mine."

"On the ones from the farm, yes," Jessie said. "But not the two Cézannes and the Seurat and the Matisse."

Sarah said, "Your word doesn't count for much against Candace Viner's."

The mask was all but off now. The fear and a raw hatred blazed in his eyes. "When did you see Candace Viner?"

"Don't you want to know how we found out about her?"

"When, damn you? When did you see her?"

"This afternoon," Jessie said.

"This afternoon. Well." The smile flickered again, but not for long.

"You're thinking the wire transfer went through yesterday, but you're wrong. It didn't. If you'd spoken to her since yesterday morning, you'd know it didn't. Something about the Cézanne aroused her suspicions. She left a message for you on Ellen Duncombe's answering machine, saying she wanted to see you again before she completed the transfer."

"Now she'll never complete it," Sarah said with relish. "No half million dollars. No sixty-four thousand dollars. No passports. No escape."

He looked at each of them in turn. Only his eyes moved; he

was hard as stone standing there, implacable, like the golem of Jewish myth. "Cunts," he said. "Goddamn smart bitch cunts."

Behold, the real Alias, Sarah thought. The slimy, poisonous thing revealed at last.

He took a step toward Morgan. "Where's the money you took from my box?"

"I told you, where you'll never get it."

"Where is it?"

"Go to hell."

"Where is it!" Another step. "Tell me, or I'll beat it out of you!"

Sarah's hand had been on her purse all along; quickly she snapped it open, dipped inside. She said, cold and sharp, "Touch her, and I'll kill you," and showed him the little .32 automatic. "I mean it, you son of a bitch. I'll shoot you dead."

Jessie

Los Alegres, California

STOP-TIME.

Thick silence, arrested motion. The threat seemed to hang in the air like smoke. From the corner of her eye Jessie could see Sarah and the gun, but most of her attention was fixed on Alias. Her reaction to him now was the same as it had been when she'd first seen him from the hallway: cold detachment and a repellent fascination, the kind of fascination she'd felt once in Philadelphia, when she and Darrin had gone to a herpatology exhibit. Unblinking, lidless eyes. Coiled, cold-blooded malevolence.

Her whole being shrank away from him, as if she'd been exposed to an uncaged bush viper or green mamba or one of the other poisonous specimens at the exhibit. Atavistic revulsion. The thought that she'd let him into her body, let herself be fucked by something reptilian, was nauseating in the extreme. She wanted him caged now more than ever, locked away where he could no longer spill his venom. Wanted it so badly that for a moment she imagined she was seeing him now through a glass wall, thick safety glass like those snake cages had been made of.

He was the one who broke the silence. "You won't shoot me," he said to Sarah.

"Won't I?"

"After all we shared together in Vancouver? I don't think so, sweet."

"Don't call me that."

"Why not? You used to like it, especially at intimate moments."

"Say it again, or take one more step, and you'll find out what I'm capable of."

"You couldn't kill any human being. It's not in you."

"You're not a human being. And it is in me. You put it there."

"Look, your hand isn't steady."

"It's steady. And the safety's off, if that's your next try to throw me off guard."

"Even if you pulled the trigger, you'd miss me," he said. "Shoot Morgan or Jessie instead."

"Not at this range. I'm a good shot, remember? You taught me how to shoot. And how to hit exactly what I'm aiming at. You see where I'm aiming right now? If you don't care about your balls, go ahead, take another step."

He tried to stare her down. Her gaze, locked with his, never wavered. There was a core of iron in Sarah, Jessie thought with admiration, forged and heated by eight years of lies and deception. She meant what she said. If he made any overt move, she would shoot him.

The staredown lasted close to half a minute, and it was Alias who broke eye contact. He shifted his gaze to Morgan, to Jessie, saw the same stony determination in their faces. Then he shrugged twice, hard shrugs, like an animal settling itself. The arrogant smile reappeared.

"All right," he said, "you win. For now."

"Go back and sit down."

"No. I'm leaving."

"You're not going anywhere."

"Yes, I am." Slowly, he turned his back to them. "As I see it," he said without moving his head, "you have two options. You can shoot me in the back, Sarah, but I don't think you're quite up to that. It's not easy to put a bullet in a man when he's walking away from you—an act of cowardice, as a matter of fact."

Jessie said, "She doesn't have to shoot you. You're one man, and there are three of us."

"That's your other option. You might manage to gang up on me, hold me here, but I promise you I'll hurt each of you in the process. As badly as I can."

On the last three words, he started away across the living room toward the dining area.

"Come back here!" Sarah shouted.

He kept walking, looking straight ahead.

She made a frustrated sound, holding the gun at arm's length. Her hand and arm, so steady before, showed tremors now.

Morgan cried, "Sarah, don't!"

In the next second Alias was in the dining room, the next after that out of sight through a doorway to the kitchen. The three of them stood rooted. In the new stillness Jessie heard the sound of a door opening, then closing again.

Sarah lowered her arm. Her face was the color of whey. "I almost did it," she whispered. "I came within a fraction of an inch. God!"

"You didn't, that's all that matters," Jessie said. "He won't get far. We'll go to the FBI right now, call Candace Viner on the way—"

Sudden noise outside.

"What was that?"

Again, louder. Somebody shouting.

Morgan said, "That came from the backyard."

Another cry, a confused series of noises.

And then, so sharp and clear it raised the hackles on Jessie's neck—a shrill, drawn-out shriek of pain.

Morgan

Los Alegres, California

THEY ran through the house and across the utility porch, Morgan leading the way. By the door was a switch for the backyard floodlights; she flipped it with one hand, yanked the door open with the other.

Two men out there, struggling, one dragging the other backward toward the gate in the fence. The gate was wide open; Alias must have come in that way, unlocking it with his key. The ground-level spots out there pinned them, showed their straining faces clearly in the windy dark.

Dalishar dragging Alias.

Alias screaming.

She stumbled through onto the porch, Jessie and Sarah crowding in close behind her. One of them said, "Oh, my God!" Other voices rose, from the Larsons' house next door, Glenn Larson shouting, "What the hell's going on over there?" Reacting, not thinking, Morgan ran down the steps and across the lawn as Dalishar pulled Alias to the gate.

"Morgan, wait!"

But she couldn't stop, and Sarah and Jessie didn't stop either; she heard their running steps behind her. Heard Alias's voice yelling, "I don't have it, there's no money . . . my arm . . . oh Jesus *you broke my arm!*"

His struggles sent Dalishar stumbling against a corner of the gate. Alias twisted loose, tried to run. Dalishar caught his arm and spun him around and hit him on the head or face, a meaty smacking impact that brought another cry of pain. Morgan was halfway across the yard by then. She saw Alias collapse in a loose huddle. Dalishar bent over him, tried to drag him upright again.

"Stop it," she shouted, "leave him alone!"

The artist's head jerked up and around. "Keep away!"

Alias started to crawl, flat on the ground, propelling himself with his knees and one arm, the other arm bent and flopping at an impossible angle. Hurt, gasping sounds bubbled out of him. Dalishar lunged forward, caught hold of one of his trouser legs. Morgan wasn't thinking clearly; in the heat of the moment she might have thrown herself at Dalishar, except that somebody— Jessie—grabbed her from behind and jerked her off to the path to one side.

Sarah ran out onto the lawn on the other side, and Morgan heard her yell, "Get away from him! I've got a gun!"

He paid no attention. He still had hold of the one leg; he heaved Alias backward through the gate.

In all the wild confusion of shouts and cries, the flat crack of the .32 was just another noise. But the effect of it was as shocking as a bomb blast. Morgan jerked as if she'd been struck, heard Jessie suck in her breath. The bullet missed Dalishar, but it came close enough to freeze him on the grassy creek bank just beyond the fence, a half-shadow with its mouth wide open. Only Alias moved, struggling to free his leg, trying to crawl again.

Sarah ran ahead, the gun extended in both hands. She didn't need to issue another command. As soon as she reached the gate, Dalishar lost his paralysis; he shouted, "Crazy bitch!" and let go of Alias's leg and went lurching out of sight along the creek bank. Morgan could hear him crashing through the berry vines that grew back there, down the bank and across the creek and into the line of eucalyptus marking the park boundary.

Alias had stopped crawling, but his legs still moved as if with a series of small seizures. Sarah got to him first, throwing the gun into one of the flower beds as she came up; Morgan and Jessie were a few steps behind her. Other people were in the yard, too, now—two or three of the neighbors.

Morgan stood looking down at him. She felt no urge to help him, no feelings for him of any kind. The other two women stood just as rigid and still. He sensed their presence and lifted his head. His face was an intaglio of pain, blood smeared across one cheek, his right eye half closed. His left arm lay twisted grotesquely at the elbow. He made an attempt to cradle it against his body, grimaced and moaned and let go again.

The neighbors came running up. One voice: "What happened? Somebody try to break in?" Another voice: "Was that a shot we heard? Hit the guy or just scare him off?" Another, Glenn Larson's: "Who's that on the ground?"

No response.

"My God, it's Burt, he's hurt . . ."

"His name isn't Burt," Morgan said.

"What?"

Alias's upward stare was glazed. "Please . . . help me, my arm . . ."

The words brought faint stirrings of sympathy, but it was the kind of impersonal compassion she would have felt for any living thing in pain. For him, the man, she still had no emotional response. He wasn't Burt, he wasn't a husband or a lover, he wasn't anybody she'd ever known. He was nothing to her. He did not exist.

She said, "Glenn, will you please call nine-eleven?"

"Sure, sure . . . right away."

One of the other neighbors said, "We'd better not try to move him. I'll get a blanket." The other neighbor took off his jacket and rolled it and knelt to put it under Alias's head.

Morgan did not want to look at him any longer; she moved a few feet away, stood hugging herself against the night's chill. Sarah and Jessie joined her. They were still standing there like that, in a tight little group, when the first siren sounded in the distance.

Late May—Early June

Jessie

Elton, Pennsylvania

H IS real name is Joseph Smith."

"You're kidding," Brenda said.

"Gospel truth, according to the Blakiston Associates detective agency."

"Joe Smith. That sounds like more of an alias than any of the ones he used!"

"Ironic, isn't it?" Jessie took another sip of her old-fashioned, tucking her legs under her on the sofa. God, it was good to be home. Five days in San Francisco, another day of meetings with John Dollarhide and Harvey Blakiston in Philadelphia. She didn't even mind Brenda's inevitable arrival and barrage of questions, though for the next three or four days she planned to play hermit—switch the phone to the answering machine and spend her time puttering around the house or attending to a couple of long-over-due restoration projects in her workroom in the barn. Peopled out. But definitely. The good, the bad, and the ugly alike.

Brenda asked eagerly, "So what's his background?"

"Born in Detroit, but he grew up in different cities across the country. Bad-genes family. His parents were both small-time con artists who traveled constantly to avoid the law. The father had a gambling habit, was always losing whatever they made from their scams. The mother was an alcoholic and a chaser. Both dead now."

"Did they use him in their con games?"

"Now and then, apparently."

"Enough for him to pick up a few pointers along the way."

"Yes, but he seems to have hated the kind of chaotic life they led. That may be the reason he stayed with each of the women he married as long as he did, why he arranged his lives with each of them along similar regimented lines—a craving for a stable home environment."

"But still he hated women."

"Love-hate feelings, I think, emphasis on hate. That's evidently the kind of relationship he had with his mother."

"Uh-huh," Brenda said. "Textbook stuff. And I'll bet she was a slender blond with small boobs."

"She was. Uneducated, foul-mouthed."

"Which is why he always picked intelligent, refined types."

"Who don't drink much if at all." Jessie took another swallow from her glass. "Except, sometimes, when the situation warrants it."

"More textbook stuff. Have they turned up his other wives yet?"

"All but one, the woman in Louisiana."

"Are they going to testify?"

"Oh, yes. The first, Doris Hatcher, was particularly eager. She caught him stealing from her while they were married and confronted him, but he disappeared before she could do anything about it."

"Faked his death?"

"Not that time. And not every other time, either. It seems to have depended on the individual woman whether or not he bothered. Doris Hatcher divorced him for desertion."

"Well, at least one of his wives wised up in time."

"Actually, that marriage wasn't strictly legal either. He was using an alias even then—Arthur Cordell."

"Why do you suppose all of his fake last names started with C-o?"

"No idea. Obviously it has some significance to him."

"Well, I can think of an obscene c-o name that fits him better than any of the others."

"So can I. Doris Hatcher, by the way, owns a small gallery in Minneapolis. He learned art appreciation from her."

"Fascinating," Brenda said, "in a gruesome sort of way. I don't suppose he's confessed yet?"

"No, and he's not likely to. He refuses to say anything to anybody except his public defender. But a confession isn't necessary. There's enough evidence to convict him on half a dozen different federal fraud counts."

"What about a murder charge?"

"He didn't kill Ellen Duncombe," Jessie said.

"He didn't? But on the phone you said he did."

"That's what we all thought at the time, despite his denials. But it turns out Dalishar was responsible. The police found her body the day after they arrested Dalishar and Serena in San Francisco—where Alias put it, in her car in a ravine three miles from the farm—and when the FBI questioned Dalishar about it, he broke down and confessed."

"Why did he kill her?"

"He swears it was an accident. It all stemmed from the Candace Viner swindle. Alias cut Dalishar out of the deal, but he couldn't do that with Ellen Duncombe; he had to tell her some of the details and promise her a cut so she would forge the Seurat and the Cézannes, the artists Candace most coveted. Duncombe must have labored long and hard over those paintings—the experts the FBI brought in agreed that they're remarkably good forgeries, by far the best of the lot."

"But Dalishar smelled a rat and flew out to California to check up."

"He found Ellen Duncombe at the farm—she'd finished the Cézanne and given it to Alias, and she was cleaning up—and forced her to tell everything she knew. Two things she didn't know were Candace's name or Alias's whereabouts, but he didn't believe her. His crazy temper made him start shaking her; she lost her balance and fell and hit her head on the concrete floor. And he panicked and ran, looking for Alias."

"So he was the one Morgan saw driving away the first time she went to the farm?"

"Yes. Right after he killed Ellen Duncombe."

"Lucky for her she couldn't get inside the building then."

"Even luckier that she didn't happen to arrive five minutes sooner. There's no telling what Dalishar might have done to her if he'd still been there."

"Brrr. Is the county going to prosecute both of them?"

"Dalishar, probably. Maybe not Alias, though; all they really have against him is unlawful disposal of a corpse. If they do prosecute Dalishar, John Dollarhide is certain there'll be a plea bargain—homicide reduced to manslaughter in exchange for Dalishar's testimony against Alias at his trial."

"Prosecution witnesses galore," Brenda said. "Maybe I'll fly out there with you and watch the parade. How long before the trial, do you think?"

"Hard to say. We don't have to be there for the arraignment, thank God. After that—a few weeks, maybe more."

"Plenty of time to regroup. For all of you."

"We're going to need it."

"You must've gotten to know Sarah and Morgan pretty well while you were together."

"About as well as we're ever likely to know one another."

"You don't plan to stay in touch with them?"

"Initially, yes. After the trial's over—I don't think so."

"Too many painful reminders?"

"And too similar in too many ways," Jessie said. "We need to put this all behind us, move on with our lives. It'll be easier to do that if we distance ourselves from each other."

"Well, you for one won't have much trouble moving on," Brenda said. "You're the strongest and most resilient woman I know, Jess. You handled losing Darrin without falling apart. This ought to be a breeze."

You don't know how close I came to falling apart, she thought. But she didn't say it. Let Brenda have her illusions. There was some truth in them anyway; she'd get through this with fewer and much more superficial scars than Darrin's death had left on her.

But Lord, she wished the damn trial was over and done with and she never again had to look at that handsome evil face.

Sarah

Okanagan Valley, British Columbia

THE valley was beautiful this time of year. Blooming orchards and green croplands along the valley floor, vineyards stretching for miles over the low fertile hills, summer people from Vancouver and Victoria and as far east as Calgary already filling the highways and resorts. The weather here was generally mild year-round, and there had been good, warm sunshine and temperatures in the mid-seventies over the past week. Watercraft made dazzling V-shaped fans on the long narrow reach of Lake Okanagan and on Lake Kalamalka at the northern end of the valley.

The cabin where she was staying was a few miles south of Vernon, high on a hillside overlooking Kalamalka. Rustic, semi-isolated, quiet. A place to heal. It was costing her nothing because it belonged to a client of David's who was spending the summer in Europe.

David had made all the arrangements. She'd let him do it in exchange for two promises. One was that he must let her pay back the remainder of his $5,000 loan—a little more than two thousand. The crooked Seattle detective who had extorted the money from her, a man named Ormond, had been exposed and arrested—one more trial that would require her eventual testimony—but only about three thousand dollars had been recovered from his apartment. The balance had already been spent. The second promise was that while she was at Kalamalka, David was not to contact her for any reason other than a major emergency. She'd been here a week now, and so far he had kept his word. She was no longer angry with him, but neither did she want his attentions. No one's attentions, for that matter. You can't begin the healing process with people around, no matter how well-intentioned, who might inadvertently keep the wounds open. In her week here, she had seen and talked to no one except a handful of tradespeople, and she meant to keep it that way for some time longer.

Later . . . well, later was later. She might go back to Vancouver, reopen the bookshop, take David in as a partner, allow him to court her and eventually marry him. Or then again, she might relocate back here. Open a smaller shop, or take a position in one of the existing bookstores, in Vernon or Kelowna. She might even take up residence in Weehaugan again for a while. She still had ties in her hometown, old acquaintances there and in other parts of the valley. It wasn't too late to reestablish her roots.

Options. For the first time since her college days, her future was wide open.

Whatever she decided, it would not be until after the trial. Between now and then, she would soak up the sun and cleanse both body and soul of contaminants. Her one concern, when she'd first arrived, was that loneliness might set in again and cause her to relapse into the bad habits of the past four years. False fear. Being alone no longer meant being lonely. Her dependency on Scotch had been an offshoot of her dependency on one man alive and dead; the end of one psychological reliance had ended the other. She had had only three drinks since she moved into the cabin, each just two fingers, each on a different night in the hour before sunset.

It was morning now, the morning of the eighth day of her stay—the most glorious so far. Warm sun, fragrant air. From the cabin's railed veranda she had a sweeping view of the treeless, grass-covered hills flanking the lake, the distant white rim of Kal Beach, the chameleon-like emerald and turquoise waters of Kalamalka itself—living up to its billing as the "Lake of a Thousand Colors." A perfect morning to sit sipping coffee and communing with all this natural beauty.

A perfect morning, too, to start writing again.

She had felt a rekindling of the creative urge the past couple of days. Such a long time since she'd had it, since she'd put words on paper. Could she write, if she were properly motivated? She thought so. Knew exactly what it was she wanted to do, including the title. Therapy. Catharsis.

Why not start now?

When she finished her coffee, she went inside and poured herself a fresh cup and then unpacked her laptop. She took both out onto the veranda, made herself comfortable on one of the woven cane chaises. Created a file, and in the middle of the first page she typed:

THE ALIAS MAN

For a few seconds she looked at the title, gathering her thoughts. Then she took a deep draught of the winy air, scrolled down to a new page, and began to write.

Morgan

San Diego, California

WHEN the doorbell rang, she was lying on the couch in her parents' front room, rereading Steinbeck's *Pastures of Heaven*. She almost didn't answer the bell. Even with the ceiling fan on—the Tepid Tollivers didn't believe in air-conditioning—it was hot and sticky in the room, and she felt lethargic. On the second ring, she sat up. If there was a third . . . There was, and she sighed and set the book aside and went to see who it was.

Alex Hazard. Wearing a tentative smile.

Some of her sleepiness fled. "Alex, for heaven's sake."

"I hope you don't mind my just dropping in like this. I called earlier, but there was no answer."

"My parents are at a seminar, and I was out shopping. No, of course I don't mind. How did you know where to find me?"

"Well, there were rumors you'd gone to stay with your folks for a while. I took the liberty of looking up their address in the school records."

"Don't tell me you came all the way to San Diego just to see me."

"Well, not exactly. Now that school's out, I'm on my annual summer driving trip to unwind." Annual since his divorce three years ago.

"I thought you drove down this way last summer."

"Two summers ago, actually. Creature of habit, that's me."

"It's good to see a friendly face," she said. "Come inside. No, it's stuffy in the house. Why don't we sit on the porch?"

"Fine."

"Beer, iced tea, soft drink?"

"Nothing, thanks. I really can't stay long."

She led him to an old-fashioned covered swing on the shady end of the porch. When they were seated he said, "How have you been, Morgan?"

"Oh, surviving."

"No better than that?"

"Long, slow process," she said. "As I don't have to tell you."

"My situation with Kia wasn't half as bad as what you went through."

"I'll get past it. Eventually."

"Sure you will." His eyes were gentle on her face. "You look well."

White lie. Hollow-cheeked, hollow-eyed, still not eating or sleeping well. But all she said was, "Right now, I could use a cold shower."

"Pretty hot, all right." He cleared his throat. "I see that you've put your house up for sale."

"There's no way I could keep on living there."

"But you will be coming back to Los Alegres? Or at least the county?"

"No, I don't think so."

It was the answer he expected. There had been a play of emotions in his face before; now the dominant one was sadness. He cleared his throat again.

"Staying here?" he asked. "In the San Diego area, I mean."

"No. There's nothing to keep me here."

"Where will you go then?"

"I don't know. I haven't really thought about it."

But she had thought about it. L.A.? San Francisco? Phoenix? One of the Pacific Northwest cities? Another small town somewhere? None of those prospects appealed to her. The truth was, no place held any appeal at the moment. Ennui. The kind of lumpishness that had nothing to do with the heat and everything to do with loose-ends boredom and stagnation. Her parents, supportive and nurturing when she'd first arrived—she'd never felt closer to them than during the first three or four days of her homecoming—had gradually reverted to their usual coolly pragmatic, tepid selves, while inside she remained as emotionally volatile and conflicted as ever. Still alive, and wanting to *be* alive again.

"I hope you'll keep in touch," Alex said, "wherever you land. Send me an e-mail now and then, or at least a Christmas card."

"Of course I will. And we'll see each other at the trial, if you're called to testify."

"I may be there even if I'm not called. Moral support."

She felt a moment of tenderness for him. "You're a good friend, Alex."

"You have more good friends than you might think. A lot of people back home have asked about you, expressed concern and support."

"Have they? I'm glad to hear it. But you came all the way down here to express yours in person."

"Least I could do. I wish I could've done more, saved you some of the grief you went through, but . . . Well, it's over with now. The worst of it."

"The worst of it."

There was a silence. He took it as a cue. "I'd best be going," he said.

"So soon?"

"Not much more to be said. But I'm glad I came. Eases my mind."

"I'm glad, too. Very."

She went with him to the porch stairs. He took her hand, held it long enough to say, "Take care of yourself, Morgan," and went quickly down the walk to his car.

She stood poised on the top step, watching him, feeling a sudden queer sensation close to loss. When he opened the car door, the sensation sharpened so painfully, it was as if something had broken loose inside.

Impulsively she called, "Alex, wait!" And when he stopped and turned, his hand on the door, she ran down to him. "Wait," she said again.

"What is it?"

"Where are you going from here? On your unwinding trip?"

"I don't know . . . down to Baja for a couple of days."

"And after that?"

"Back up the coast. No specific plans. Why?"

"Highway One? Hearst Castle, Big Sur?"

"Morgan, what—"

"Take me with you," she said.

His quizzical expression became one of astonishment. "You're not serious."

"Completely serious. I've always wanted to visit Hearst Castle, I haven't been to Big Sur in years, there are a lot of places I've never seen and things I've never done, and there's no reason on earth I couldn't see and do some of them with you. Is there?"

"No, but . . . just like that, just pick up and go?"

"Right now. I'll leave my folks a note. They won't mind."

"But traveling together . . . accomodations . . ."

"We'll work that out. That's not an issue."

"Morgan . . ." He shook his head. "And when the trip's over, what then?"

"I may go back to Los Alegres with you. Perhaps that's where I belong after all. Or I may say good-bye and move on somewhere else, I don't know yet. No specific plans. One day at a time."

"Are you sure you want to do this?"

Always conservative, never spontaneous. Always "doing the right thing," the expected thing, the conventional thing. Always living in a trap built of the unseen and the unknown and shored up with what-ifs and afraid-tos, never simply running free. The Tepid Tollivers had been right about one thing: You really did have to take control of the situation, do what was best for you, your peace of mind, your survival.

"I've never been more sure of anything in my life," she said.